Surviving My Happy Childhood

Stories by
Jim Carpenter

delicti
press

Surviving My Happy Childhood

Copyright ©2010 Jim Carpenter

ISBN 978-0-9798526-5-7

LCCN 2010929299

Delicti Press
Northport, Michigan
editor@delictipress.com

This is a work of fiction. Names, characters, places and incidents are either products of the author's imagination or are used fictitiously.

Publisher's Cataloging-in-Publication
    Carpenter, Jim
        p.cm.
        ISBN: 978-0-9798526-5-7

        1. Surviving My Happy Childhood: Stories/Jim Carpenter
        2. Michigan Author
        3. Carpenter, Jim
        4. Short Stories, Midwest

In Memory of Luther and Louise Carpenter

Acknowledgements
I would like to thank Larry Brand, Patricia Fabian,
Rebecca Reynolds, Jeffra Rockwell, Robert Underhill,
and Trudy Underhill for their invaluable
contributions to this book.

Special thanks go to Rebecca for her
love, humor, and support.

Surviving My Happy Childhood

1.	The Cloak Room Incident	1
2.	Tiger Baseball	9
3.	Catch a Wave	27
4.	Boys' State	33
5.	In My Room	41
6.	Big Dog on Campus	45
7.	Listen to This	53
8.	Paris Peace Talks	59
9.	A Day of Firsts	67
10.	Open Wide	73
11.	Coleville of the Dale	81
12.	Depresso's Lists	89
13.	Respecting Privacy	97
14.	E.V.A.N.S.	105
15.	Sammy	115
16.	Sing Praises Unto Our King	121
17.	Down Five With Six Minutes to Go	127
18.	Arthur Woodridge	133
19.	Time Off	139
20.	Now!	143

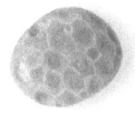

The Cloak Room Incident

It was the perfect throw. Not surprising though. Danny had a great arm and threw hard and accurately. He was the king of winter recess. Only one problem.

That particular snowball "accidentally" hit our third grade teacher, Mrs. Warren, in the back of the head. Accidentally. Right.

Mrs. Warren staggered forward but quickly regained her composure and spun around to face her enemy. Considering her age, size, and physical condition, it was a very impressive maneuver.

Her icy cold eyes locked in on the two of us. "You two. Come with me. Now!"

Danny could have, hell, should have done the right thing. He should have run up to her and said, "I did it, Mrs. Warren. It was my fault, and I take full responsibility. Stanley had nothing to do with it." He didn't do that, though. In his defense, not many eight-year-olds would have.

Instead, he put his arm around me, a huge, almost demonic grin on his face, and directed us as one guilty entity forward to our certain death. Comrades in arms.

Equally guilty.

I knew what it must have looked like to Mrs. Warren. The two of us had plotted the whole thing together. Neither one of us was going to squeal. We were united. We were blood brothers. We weren't afraid of her. We were challenging her, daring her to do something.

She couldn't have been more wrong. I was terrified. So terrified I don't remember the forced march back inside the school. Mrs. Warren let our classmates put their things in the cloakroom at the back of the class-room and then told Danny and me to "go in there and think about what you have done."

The cloakroom was a long, narrow, dark closet. Maybe 20 feet long and eight feet wide. The two long walls were separated into individual cubbies, deep enough to crawl back into. Each cubby had three hooks for hanging coats and, in winter, leggings, scarves, gloves, you name it. And there were little stoops under each cubbyhole for boots and shoes.

We just barely had time to get to our cubbies when Mrs. Warren turned off the lights. The room was pitch dark. I sat down and took off my coat and boots. It was incredibly hot.

I wasn't talking to Danny. I was really pissed off at him for dragging me into this. I just crawled into my cave.

After about 15 minutes, I fell asleep. Mrs. Warren had forgotten about us.

Next thing I knew, the lights came back on, the door opened and in came Betsy Thornberg. She was holding a bag with something in it. She walked over to her cubby and started undressing, totally oblivious to our presence.

Later we found out that Betsy had had an "accident" after coming in from recess. Her mother had dutifully brought Betsy a change of clothes. And Mrs. Warren had sent Betsy into the cloakroom to change without giving it a second thought.

Peeking out from our cubby cave openings, Danny and I witnessed a strip tease show, seven-year-old style.

I sneezed just as she finished undressing. One of my more explosive sneezes. Betsy screamed. Danny burst into laughter, and Mrs. Warren let out a blood-curdling cry that said loud and clear she knew she'd screwed up.

Instead of fleeing (she was naked after all), Betsy crawled into her cubby cave to cover up behind her coat and leggings. For all she knew, we were gonna kill her. She wasn't about to find out by asking.

Within five seconds, a livid Mrs. Warren came bursting into the room, ignoring Betsy for the moment and directing her furor at the two convicts.

"Get out! Get out! You are going to the principal's office. Now!"

She catapulted us out into the hallway, turned to the other students without saying anything to Betsy and shouted, "Continue with your work sheets. And I don't want to hear a peep out of any of you! Linda, you're in charge. Take down the name of anyone who misbehaves."

We didn't wait for Mrs. Warren. We high-tailed it for

the office as quickly as we could, without running in the hallways of course. We didn't need another felony charge on top of our pending attempted murder charge.

Mrs. Warren moved surprisingly fast (she must've run…I wasn't looking back) and was right behind us by the time we got to the principal's office.

Danny opened the door and, showing his best manners, offered to hold it for her, but Mrs. Warren stood firmly in place, guarding the doorway from a possible breakaway attempt.

Pointing to the two empty chairs just inside the room, Mrs. Warren commanded, "You sit right there and don't move. Don't talk. Don't do anything. You hear me?"

I nodded and looked over at Danny. He didn't react. She knocked on Principal Donovan's door, opened it, entered, and slammed it behind her.

Mr. Donovan's secretary, seated across from us at her desk, had snapped-to when we entered. She gave us a quick look that said, "Been nice knowing you," and then pretended to bury herself in paperwork. I wasn't buying it since I'd seen her doing her nails when we walked in.

At this point I knew I should have been seriously weighing my options, but my mind was totally blank. My conviction was imminent. Now it was just a question of how I was going to die. The headline in our local paper would read "Second Graders Go To The Chair For Heinous Crimes."

I was no longer thinking about Danny. It was all

about personal survival now, and that looked pretty bleak. My word against a teacher's? No one would believe me. I didn't have a prayer.

If I wanted to avoid execution, let alone be allowed to stay in this school system, I would have to throw myself on the mercy of the court. Admit guilt and take my punishment like a man.

We sat there for five minutes. It felt like an hour. We didn't say a thing. The one time I glanced over at Danny, he seemed relaxed, almost self-assured. When the principal's door opened, Mr. Donovan was standing there and, with a simple, powerful flick of his finger, motioned us into his inner sanctum.

There were two empty seats in the room beside Mrs. Warren. Danny immediately walked over and sat down right next to her. Fine with me.

Mr. Donovan got right to the point. "Well boys, what do you have to say for yourselves?"

No response, so he continued.

"Mrs. Warren tells me you…"

I opened my mouth to say something like, "It's all my fault. I'll never do it again." The ultimate guilty plea by an innocent bystander hoping to save his life.

Danny beat me to it.

"Mr. Donovan, I don't think you have any idea what Stanley and I have just been through. We haven't done anything wrong. In fact we're the ones who've been mistreated." He stopped for effect.

It was brilliant. I was instantly in awe of Danny. He had obviously been plotting this from the moment we went into the cloakroom. He had real street smarts.

Mr. Donovan was caught completely off guard. He'd been blind-sided. His look of controlled, absolute power had transformed instantaneously into a look of total bewilderment. He'd never been in this position before. His faculty members were always right. The students were always guilty. The only thing he had to do in these situations was pronounce judgment. Something he enjoyed immensely.

He threw a quick glance in Mrs. Warren's direction as if to say, "What have you gotten me into, you bitch." A look of horror had come over her. The next line was hers. "I can't believe..."

Danny interrupted her. "I can't believe it either. Mrs. Warren threw us into the cloakroom, yelled at us, turned off the lights, and slammed the door just like she did when she came in this room a few minutes ago. She left us alone in that dark, scary, steaming cell. And then, obviously, she forgot about us. Let me repeat that. She forgot about us."

Turning to her, Danny, now shaking all over, put the nail in the coffin, "Didn't you, Mrs. Warren?"

Danny had been preparing his entire life for this moment, and he was going all out!

Mr. Donovan and Mrs. Warren were speechless. Danny kept right on going. "Do you know what it's like? Put yourself in our shoes. Just imagine what Betsy thinks of us?" Another pause for effect, "The rest of our classmates are going to label us as misfits. We'll be outcasts for sure."

Danny realized he'd said enough. He reached over and put his arm around me. I've always been able to cry on cue, so I let loose with some classic sobbing. And it was all over. Danny squeezed my shoulder to recognize my important contribution to the moment.

Mr. Donovan shook his head. His day, perhaps his year (maybe even his career depending on what Danny did next), had just gone to hell. He did the only thing he could do. He stood up, looked directly at Mrs. Warren and said, "You owe them an apology." And then to us, he added, "Though I do not condone your behavior at recess, I do believe that Mrs. Warren made a poor choice." He shook his head and continued. "No, I mean unfortunate choice, back in the classroom." And then he looked again at Mrs. Warren.

She quickly mumbled something to the floor about being sorry, about using poor judgment, and that it wouldn't happen again.

Danny stood. I did, too.

Mr. Donovan rapped his right fist on his desk. "Excellent. Now let's get back to class. And not a word of what's been said here leaves this room. Do I make myself perfectly clear?" He looked at the two of us.

I nodded yes vigorously. Danny did not, as if to say, "stay tuned, this is not over yet." Mr. Donovan knew what it meant, but he wasn't about to pursue it and risk escalation.

"Thank you. You may leave."

We started to walk toward the door. Danny put his arm around me and whispered, "I thought that went very well. Now, I think you should cry just a little bit more for effect. Just to put the icing on the cake."

I was on the verge of crying anyways and was only too happy to oblige. They were ours, or rather, they were Danny's, and they knew it.

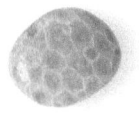

Tiger Baseball

I was supposed to mow my backyard today. I had my Stroh's chilling in the cooler in anticipation of the successful completion of this male ritual. And my radio was sitting on the patio table next to my lawn chair.

I have to admit, there's nothing like popping a cold beer and flopping back in a chair to listen to the Tigers, celebrating baseball with the smell of freshly cut grass. If I try hard enough, I can almost believe I'm at the corner of Michigan and Trumbull, standing outside Briggs Stadium moments before another great home game.

Before coming outside I heard George Kell say on WWJ that it was raining in Detroit and that the game with the Chicago White Sox "might be canceled. "If so, we'll play two tomorrow, friends." Then, to make matters worse, my lawn mower wouldn't start. Plenty of gas. The blade assembly wasn't clogged with grass. Oil level looked good, and I'd changed the plug earlier in the summer. The damn thing just wouldn't start. Two strikes.

Just then I heard those wonderful words, "The Tigers take the field." I turned to see a tennis ball ricochet off the back of the Sisson house and heard the Sisson boy, Mac, proudly announce, "It's a beautiful day for baseball, ladies and gentlemen. Not a cloud in the sky."

And he was right. It was a beautiful day for baseball in our sunny neighborhood 220 miles west of Detroit. "Tiger baseball is on the air."

Mac continued, "First, for the visiting Chicago White Sox, here is today's lineup. Leading off and playing centerfield is Jim Landis. Batting second and playing second base is Nellie Fox. Luis Aparicio is at short and will bat third. Roy Sievers is batting cleanup and playing first. Gene Freese is in the five spot at third, followed by Minnie Minoso in left, Al Smith in right, Sherm Lollar behind the plate, and Billy Pearce on the mound. For our Tigers, it'll be Kaline, Bruton, and Colavito in the outfield, Cash on first, Wood on second, Fernandez at short, Boros at third, Brown behind the plate, and Mr. Reliable, Frank Lary, doing the pitching." I was surprised to hear Lary's name. He was scheduled to go against the Yankees on Sunday in the second game of the doubleheader. It was stupid to pitch him this early in the season on only two days rest, especially when he was unbeatable against the Yankees.

And then I heard the explanation. "Lary's coming off two days rest but, with Bunning out and Foytack's blister on his pitching hand, Scheffing needs Frank today. That's the kind of player Frank Lary is. He'll sacrifice anything for the team. Scheffing's just hoping he can get five good innings out of him."

This kid is one heck of an announcer. He is better at the age of ten than most of the big league announcers ever are. He has the sense to borrow the best mannerisms and catch-phrases of George Kell and Ernie Harwell. Where does a kid like this pick it up? One thing's for sure. Practice makes perfect. He's out here nearly every day for at least an hour. Throwing the ball and calling the games.

I had a tough choice to make. Go take the lawn mower over to Vander Ploeg Repair or stay here and listen to my ten-year old neighbor do the play-by-play of the Tiger-White Sox game that had been rained out in Detroit. I was snapped back to reality with Mac finishing his impression of sexy Julie London, "...you get a lot to like with a Marlboro. Filter, flavor, pack or box." I forgot to tell you. Mac does commercials, too. And that's not all. He sings "America, the Beautiful" before the game starts, obviously preferring it to the "Star Spangled Banner."

OK, I admit it. I listen to Mac's games every chance I get.

The Sissons have the house due north of ours. Our backyards are separated by a small, rickety picket fence on the northwest border and by a tall row of bushes and young trees on the northeast border. In between is an overgrown three-foot wide path connecting the two yards. It doesn't get used much...by adults. In Mac's make-believe world, however, anything that goes over the fence or bushes on the fly is a home run. Makes sense to me. He uses the path to retrieve the homers or occasional ground-rule double.

There's a brick patio right off their back door with a knee-high cinder block ledge on the south and east sides. Then there's a 50 by 50 foot open space that separates the patio from the fence. It's this open space where Mac stands to throw the ball off the south wall of their house, a wall with two upstairs windows and a lower shed roof protruding over the walkway. Their yard extends west of the open space for another 50 feet easy. Mac chases a lot of foul balls over that way.

"Lary's done with his warm-ups! Sit back and enjoy the game, folks!" A ball came bouncing into our yard, and Mac bolted through the connector path to retrieve it. Seeing me, he slammed on the brakes (almost knocking his Tiger hat off his head) and instantaneously switched to a relaxing stroll. "Hi, Dr. Waldrop. Sorry about the ball," he said as he bent down to pick it up. "Not to worry, Mac. Game today?" "Yes sir," he replied as he turned and walked back to the path and then exploded onto the field.

Without giving it a second thought, I walked over to my cooler, got out a Stroh's and sat down in my patio chair. Mac had done his homework. The Sox, not known for their power, singled, doubled, walked, and stole their way for three runs off Lary in the top of the first. It looked like a long day for Detroit and a short one for Lary. Scheffing got Reagan up to throw in the bullpen, and I thought for a second he might pull Lary as soon as Reagan was warmed up. That way Lary might still be available for a stint on the mound on Sunday. But Bruton robbed Lollar of a sure double and two more runs with a great running catch to get the Tigers out of the inning.

The Tigers went down in order in the bottom of the first, and the White Sox pitcher, Billy Pierce, who Mac reminded his listeners was a native Michigander, promptly doubled to start off the Sox second. It was all I could do not to yell, "Pull him, Scheffing!" Just then I heard a scream and Mac announced, "He's out! Lary just picked Pierce off second. Billy got caught leaning and never had a chance. Great play!" And, for good measure, he added, "Scheffing was standing on the edge of the dugout. Lary may have just been one pitch away from an early shower. Now Scheffing's moved back to the bench."

This kid knows the game inside out. He's got a good speaking voice. And he has that unique ability to pull his listeners in – to make the broadcast so real that you feel like you're right there. Just like the greats. Ah, the wonder of radio.

Lary got Landis and Fox on routine fly balls, though Fox's went off the Sisson's shed roof overhang and a hundred or so feet up in the air before Mac hauled it in on the warning track.

According to Mac, Colavito fouled off five straight pitches in a row to start off the Tiger half of the second and then slapped a single in the hole between short and third. Cash sacrificed Colavito to second, and Boros got the first Tiger RBI with a single to the opposite field

("The Tigers are on the board, ladies and gentlemen!").
I thought Smith would throw to the plate, but he went
to second instead to keep Boros on first. Good call by
Mac...one run is no big deal this early.

Then Minoso made a superb catch at the wall to rob
Wood of a sure-bet home run. Brown walked to put
runners on first and second with two out. Lary was the
batter and, true to form, singled Boros home with the
second Tiger run. Mac knew Lary was the best hitting
pitcher in the American League and took advantage of
it. Fernandez grounded out to Aparicio to end the inning.

The Sox got two more runs off Lary in the third.
Scheffing had to get Reagan back up in the bullpen,
this time with Burnside joining him. I was pretty upset with Lary. He served up a fastball on a platter for
Smith as if he had no idea Smith was a fastball hitter.
I found myself agreeing with some boos coming from
the announcer's voice.

Somehow Lary settled down and pitched the fourth,
fifth, and sixth innings very effectively. The highlight
during that stretch was an early 7th inning stretch (in
the sixth) when both of us had to relieve ourselves. The
Tigers had stranded six more runners and still trailed
5-2 as Lary took the mound in the 7th. Mac was quick
to point out that Frank looked a little tired in the 6th
and had gotten away with hanging a couple of fast
balls up in the strike zone. Lollar and Pierce led the
inning off with back-to-back singles and then the announcer said, "Here comes Scheffing to the mound.
That's going to do it for Lary this afternoon. Not one

of his best outings this year. Even so, he gets a warm round of applause from the home crowd as he heads for the Tiger dugout."

Scheffing signaled down to the bullpen for a right hander who had not yet been identified. Then came the announcement, "The new pitcher is Mac Sissons. Just called up from Toledo." He obviously had a big fan club at the park, because he got a very warm reception. "He's a tall, lanky right-hander. You folks in Grand Rapids will remember him for the two no-hitters he pitched at East High. He went on to be a star at the University of Michigan and was signed by the Tigers when he graduated. While he warms up, let's take a break. You're listening to WWJ, the home of the Detroit Tigers."

And off we went to an Ipana Toothpaste commercial, sung all the way through by Mac, "brusha, brusha, brusha, new Ipana Toothpaste..."

After another Stroh's commercial, Mac was back on the air. "This is Sisson's first year in the bigs. Before being called up last week, he was 5-1 with Toledo and had an E.R.A. of 2.84. His best pitch is a hard slider that breaks equally well to both right and left-handed batters. He's got an average fastball and an above average curveball and change-up." And then, as an afterthought, Mac added, "Sisson could be a pleasant surprise for the Tigers this year. They sure could use someone else coming out of the bullpen."

It was a tough spot for a rookie. First and second, no one out, and Jim Landis at the plate. Everyone listening at home knew Landis was deadly in situations like this. Fortunately, he popped up the first pitch, and Boros caught it in foul territory right next to the third base bag. (The ball hit the attic window ledge and shot way up in the air. I'm not sure whether Mac actually caught it, because there was a time lapse of a few seconds before the announcer called Landis out.) Fox hit a slow dribbler to Wood at second, and Wood's only play was to first. Two out and the runners had moved up to second and third. Then Sisson walked Aparicio to load the bases. "Here comes Scheffing to the mound. Is this it for Sisson? He's done a good job so far, but the skipper may have decided to bring on the leftie, Hank Aguirre, to pitch to Sievers. Brown has come out there, too, and Fernandez has come in to join them from short."

I was hoping to see Sisson stay in and, sure enough, Mac said, "Scheffing has decided to leave Sisson in there. He obviously reminded Sisson how to pitch to Sievers and is now trotting back to the dugout." Another pause and then, "Well here goes. Sisson shakes off the sign from Brown, now nods approval of the second sign, checks off the runners and here's the pitch. Ball up high. Sisson looks around the infield and now steps back in. Sets. And here's the windup and the pitch. Fly ball down the leftfield line. It's...it's... it's curving foul." It was more than I could take. I was up on our patio ledge and saw the ball come off the second story window at a weird angle. It looked like a fair ball to me, but it had obviously fooled Mac and caught him leaning the wrong way. He had no chance to make the catch and so, wisely, called it a foul ball. To cover it up a little more, the announcer added, "That was a close one folks. That ball was well hit. Sievers was guessing fastball all the way. Sisson rubs the new ball and now steps back on the rubber. One ball and one strike. And here's the pitch. Ground ball back to the pitcher. Sisson fields it cleanly, turns, and throws to first for the out. Sievers was way out in front of that big-league change-up. And Sisson pitches out of a real jam. The Sox strand runners on second and third. So, after seven and one half innings, it's still the White Sox 5 and the Tigers 2."

Now that's relief pitching at its best. You could feel the momentum change right then and there. The Sox had had their chance to put the game out of reach and couldn't take advantage of it. I jumped down from the patio ledge and went over to get another Stroh's from the cooler. When I hurried back to the ledge, Mac was putting the finishing touches on a Cheerios commercial ("...he's got go-power!").

"It'll be Wood, Brown, and Sisson in the Tiger 7th." Mac had made his first mistake. It was supposed to be Bruton, Kaline, and Colavito, but I knew it was now or never, so I had no problem with his decision. "If the Tigers hope to pull this one out, they're going to have to find a way to get to Pierce. Billy has been unhittable since the second inning." Pierce proceeded to throw two high fastballs in a row. Then, "The wind-up and the pitch. That ball is well hit. Minoso's going back to the wall and...he makes the catch. Just a little more and Jake would have had his third round-tripper of the year." And, sure enough, Mac made a nifty catch right up against the picket fence that would have made Minnie proud. Those are tough balls to throw...to hit the house just right to make it go that far...and then make the catch, too! Though it looked to me like one of his dad's roses had been a casualty of the great play.

"Brown's up. He's been on a hitting streak lately and has two of the Tiger five hits today." And then the toughest part of broadcasting...when you're the announcer and the batter on deck is you. "If Brown gets on, I think we'll see a pinch hitter for Sisson. Ground ball. Easy play for Aparicio. Two up. Two down. And now Scheffing has a tougher choice. Sisson pitched well in the 7th and, according to his AAA stats, is a pretty good hitter. He's coming back to the dugout now. Will it be Charlie Maxwell?" And then there was about a five second "dead air" delay before the announcer spoke again, "Sisson is going to bat. I don't know if I agree with that one, Ernie." That was the first time Mac had recognized another announcer in the booth...Ernie Harwell.

"Sisson's a leftie at the plate. They used him to pinch hit a fair amount in Toledo. Here's the first pitch from Pierce. Oh! High and tight. Nearly hit him, Ern!" My beer was nearly gone already. I wanted to charge the mound and deck Mr. Pierce. What gives him the right to throw at our fine rookie's head?

"Sisson steps back out of the box. Takes a couple of

practice swings. Now he's back in. And here comes the pitch. It's a hit! Down the right field line. Could be two. Sisson's digging for second. Here comes the throw from Smith and it's...too late! A stand-up double for Sisson. This kid can run, folks. There's no way Scheffing will pinch-run for that speed. Well, here comes Fernandez. Last time up he hit one a mile foul. Sisson takes a big lead on second. Two out. Here's the pitch. Line shot to center. It's in there for a hit. Here comes Sisson, and he'll score easily. Chico's on first, and the Tigers have narrowed the Sox lead to 5-3." I caught myself just before I started to yell. These Tigers are something else. All year they've done this. Come back from two or three runs down to win a nail biter.

"Lopez has Lown and Wynn, both right-handers, loosening up in the bullpen. Pierce is obviously tiring. And here comes Lopez out of the dugout. Taking his sweet time walking to the mound, too. He wants to give his two relief artists a chance to get better limbered up. He's saying a few words to Pierce and his battery mate, Lollar, and is now heading slowly back to the dugout. Bruton steps in."

I know Mac. I know Tiger baseball. And I knew what was about to happen. I had just enough time to jump off the patio ledge and run to the fence and pretend to be weeding when I heard the announcer scream, "Billy got all of it! It could be...yes, it's going, going...gone! A two-run homer for Billy Bruton, and we're all tied up!" And, sure enough, the tennis ball came flying right over my head, bounced on my thick, unmowed grass, and came to a stop in the middle of my lawn. Mac came flying into my yard still mimicking the crowd cheers and continuing the play-by-play. "This crowd is going bonkers, ladies and gentlemen! And Lopez is making the slow walk to the mound. He should have pulled Pierce, and he knows it. Tiger fans, we have a brand new ballgame!"

Mac never saw me at all. He was so focused on that home run and what might happen next that he ran right by me. Sure enough, Lopez brought on Lown to pitch to Kaline, Mac's favorite Tiger (and mine). But Mac kept his cool. Al hit a pop fly to Landis in center to end the inning. That took a lot. It was a perfect Kaline moment. "But not before the Tigers strike for three and tie this thing up." And then, as an afterthought, "Let's not forget who got this rally going...the young right-hander from Grand Rapids...Mac Sisson. Time out for a Stroh's."

At this point, Mac moved the game to his driveway. He had to because he actually pitched out there (using the garage door handle as a target) and stood what looked to me to be the official distance away from "home plate." I could occasionally make out a word or two if I snuck into his yard but nothing significant. One inning was about all he ever pitched out there, so I patiently weeded along the fence while I waited for him to return. It never crossed my mind that I was weeding some of my wife's parsley.

Sure enough, ten minutes later, Mac returned to the backyard for the ninth inning. The score, according to the announcer, was still 5-5. Sisson had obviously done his job. Apparently, however, the Tigers hadn't done anything in their half of the inning either. Both of us knew who was coming up for Chicago. Landis, Fox, and Aparicio.

It didn't start well. Landis doubled to right center. But then Sisson buckled down and got Fox to pop up to Wood behind second. On the play, Mac ran in hard and obviously collided with the patio ledge. He went down hard after making the catch, and it was a good three or four minutes before play resumed. I think he was crying, but I know for a fact that he made the catch.

Sisson got Aparicio to fly out to Colavito in left. Two out and Sievers up. One for three and an RBI in today's game. A hit here would be a sure run. And everyone in the park knew Landis would be running on anything hit. Sisson's first two pitches to Sievers, both balls, high and outside, didn't bode well for us either. Then the call. "A shot to right. Kaline's coming on, but it's going to drop. Here comes Landis around third. He's being waved home. Kaline's going to the plate. Here comes the throw, and it's on the money. This is going to be really close. Landis slides. He's..."

A very tough decision for Mac. Does Kaline get him or do the Sox score and go up one? I never doubted Mac's next words. After all, we're talking about Al Kaline here! "He's out at the plate! Out at the plate! Can you believe that throw by Kaline? A one-hopper right to Brown. Only a perfect throw could have cut down the speedy Landis. And this crowd is going wild."

I had a perfect view of the whole play. Mac cleanly fielded the ball off the lower part of the wall and came up throwing. Low. So low that he came within an eyelash of hitting his back door and his dad's grill on the rebound. He really had something on that throw, too. The ball bounced back on one hop and Mac (now playing Brown) put a perfect tag on Landis and then jumped in the air to show the umpire he was still holding the ball. Magical. Sisson ran into the Tiger dugout at full speed.

We were both set for the last of the ninth. Colavito, Cash, and Boros due up. "Sisson's done all he can do, and now it's up to his teammates. Juan Pizarro has come on to pitch for the White Sox. For those of you keeping score at home, Lown went one and one-third innings in relief. Well, Rocky is 1-3 today. He finishes his characteristic bat-behind-the-back bend and steps into the batter's box. And here's the pitch. It's a bunt! And he's caught Freese totally by surprise at third. If it stays fair, it's gonna be a hit. And it does! Oh, my goodness, Ernie. I can't remember the last time Colavito bunted! Was that Scheffing's decision or did Colavito decide to do it on his own? What a great, great call."

It really was. Mac had definitely outdone himself with this one. On the bunt, I jumped to my right along the fence line, intently following the path of the imaginary ball as if to make sure it stayed fair. Man, the White Sox are in trouble now. No outs and a runner on first!

"That's not Pizarro's fault. That was a big league play

made by a big league player. Rocky looks like he's got a grin on his face as he takes a short lead off first. Cash is up. All we need is a sacrifice, Norm. The infield is drawn in to make the force at second. Pizarro checks the runner. And here's the pitch. No. Throw to first and Colavito is back just in time. Here we go again. The set. And the pitch. Ground ball to Aparicio. To Fox for one and back to first. Safe. The throw pulled Sievers off the bag, and Cash is safe at first. I've never seen Norm run that fast to first in all my years of broadcasting! One out and Boros is up. He's 0 for 3 today, but he's got a couple of fielding gems to his credit. He's due, Ernie."

"That he is, pahdna." Mac had answered in Dizzy Dean's voice without thinking.

Pizarro walked Boros on four pitches. Runners on first and second. One out. And that was all for Pizarro. The Colavito bunt had really shaken him up. According to Mac, Lopez bolted out of the dugout and signaled to the bullpen for his reliever, veteran Early Wynn.

The phone rang inside my house but I let it ring. I wasn't going to miss this for anything.

After giving Wynn enough time to complete his warm-ups, Mac continued, "It's Wynn against Wood. Jake is 0 for 3 but has nearly hit two out of here today. A base hit will win this game. The outfield is cheating in a little bit for a potential play at the plate. And here we go. Ball one. Low and away. Wynn, a sure thing for the Hall of Fame, is primarily a screwball/fast-ball pitcher. The wind-up and the pitch. Just missed. Wood's got a great eye. Wynn thought that one got the corner though and isn't too happy about the call."

Oh yeah. Bring it on. Mac was killing me.

"Wood will be taking this one all the way. And here it is. Ball three. High and outside. I wouldn't be surprised if Wynn gets the signal to intentionally walk Wood at this point. You can bet yourself one thing. Wood will be taking all the way again. The sign from Lollar. And here's the pitch. SMACK! That ball is well hit. It's going to go over Minoso's head to the wall. Cash will score easily. The Tigers win! Who would have thought Colavito would bunt and that Wood would swing away on a 3-0 count! Unbelievable! And this crowd is going nuts. The Tiger players are mobbing Jake, and right in the middle of that mob is young Mac Sisson. This is his first major league win, Ernie."

"It sure is. And I like the look of this kid. I think he's got a bright future in a Tiger uniform. So the Tigers win this one, 6-5. Back with the totals in 60 seconds."

The ball had bounced into my yard on the hop. Mac came running past me beaming from ear to ear. At that moment I'm sure he could have scaled a tall building in a single bound. I really had no time to react, but he never saw me. I'll never forget that look on his face.

I turned away from the ballpark and pushed my broken lawn mower around to the front of the house. I was still in disbelief. What a great game! Just then I heard Jack Roberts, a neighbor from down at the end of the block, "Hey Ed, did the Tigers play today?" Jack asked me every day rain or shine. Still in a daze I responded, "Tigers just won 6-5!" And Jack replied, "Really? I thought they were going to get rained out."

As I returned to the backyard to get my cooler and empties, I heard those magical words, "The final today, Detroit 6, Chicago 5. The losing pitcher, Juan Pizzaro. And the winner, Mac Sisson, with his first major league victory. What a game! This is the Detroit Tiger baseball network. See you tomorrow, Ernie. It'll be Gary Peters on the mound for the White Sox and Don Mossi for the Tigers. Pregame show at 1:30 and game time 2:00. Thanks for tuning in."

I'll be there. Let me rephrase that. I'll be here.

Catch A Wave

R eece got us started doing it. For all I know, he invented it.

Mark interviewed him for the school paper. Mark was a renegade and was willing to write anything to get a rise out of the administration and teachers. It usually worked. He liked interviewing Reece. Everything Reece said (and did) was controversial.

Mark: Describe the rush you get, "Sam." (Mark always tried to protect the privacy of his sources. It never worked.)

Reece: The Beach Boys said it best. "Catch a wave and you're sittin' on top of the world."

Mark: So, bumper hitching is the Midwest equivalent of surfing?

Reece: And just as dangerous. Maybe even more so.

Mark: How long have you been doing it?

Reece: Started last winter.

Mark: Where did you get the idea?

Reece: I don't sleep much, so I have lots of time to think about things.

That's all it took. The day after the paper came

out, Officer Duncan showed up at school to talk to "Sam," who he knew had to be Reece. Seems he was concerned about others trying bumper hitching and getting horribly maimed.

The peace and quiet of Officer Duncan's tiny hamlet went to hell overnight. The "talk" didn't work.

Reece became an instant folk hero. Kids from other schools even called him at home to ask for pointers. He spent most of his spare time driving around town scouting out the best bumper hitching streets. All our friends at school started talking surfer talk. And the record store sold out of the Beach Boys' album *Surfin' USA* in two days. Rex Carmichael even got tossed out of Mrs. Madison's English class for singing at the top of his lungs, "Tell the teacher I'm surfin', surfin' USA." We weren't sure if he got the boot for his terrible voice or the message of rebellion and impending revolution.

Reece really got into the surfing/bumper hitchin' comparisons. He would hold court before study hall, sharing all the surfing lingo that could be transposed to bumper hitchin'. Wipeout. Surf's up. Dude this, dude that. Shooting the pipe. A couple of freshmen even peroxided their hair. Hero worship had begun in earnest.

True to form, Reece saved his best mentoring for his closest friends. On the way to school in the morning. At lunch hour. On the phone at night. "It's gotta be tennis shoes, man. Smooth surface. Faster than shit when the conditions are right. Like waxin' up your board, man!" Or, "Knee pads, man. You gotta wear knee pads."

I got the call on Thursday night at 7:30. When the

phone rang, I knew who it was.

"Surf's up! Oak Street in half an hour. In front of Rockwell's house."

"What about the geometry test tomorrow?"

"There will be other geometry tests. The waves can't wait."

"You're nuts, man!"

"I'm maxed, man!" And then he threw me another Brian Wilson lyric, "We're waxin' down our surfboards, can't wait til--." He hung up before the lyric stopped working. The next word was "June."

He was right of course. The conditions were perfect. It had sleeted late in the afternoon. Dad had even commented on how slippery it was on his way home from work. And then it started to snow. A thick, powdery snow. Not too wet. Two to three inches easy. Packed down by the cars. We couldn't have asked for anything more.

Reece knew I'd show. Booney and Finn were there, too. Reece said he would solo the first ride to check out the road conditions. Make sure everything was just right. Appease the gods. Just then a GTO turned the corner onto Oak St. heading right for us. Reece was standing in the driveway and got a running start, perfectly timed to hook up with the GTO as it passed us. He effortlessly grabbed onto the back bumper, adjusted his grip, and waved to us as he disappeared around the bend.

About four minutes later, he came running back, fists raised, jumping up and down for joy. Covered in snow.

"Unbelievable, man! Perfect waves. I was hangin' five at one point!"

Trying to sound hip, Booney said, "Did you wipe out, man?"

"Man, I hit the last bend. Right there at Samuelson's house. The dude must have known I was on. He goosed it, and I went flying off into Hibbard's yard. So cool."

And then Finn let loose with this blood curdling scream, his way of saying, "Gentlemen, start your engines."

We were totally stoked. Just as we were about to "hit the surf" with Reece, we saw Mark Thomas coming down the street. Typical. Reece had called him, too, and told him to come out and see for himself how cool bumper hitchin' was. Mark saw it as his big chance. This was the story that would be picked up by the *AP*, propelling him into instant stardom.

We "hitched" for about a half hour. Several good rides. A couple of great wipeouts, but no serious injuries. Then, Reece asked Mark and me to join him for a "triple trouble." Three on one bumper. Unheard of in the bumper hitching literature.

Later, Sammy Stephens said he could tell by the jerk in the back of his Camaro when we hooked on. Off we went. The ultimate ride. Reece had told Mark to hold on no matter what, and he did a great job. That is, until the last straightaway before coming to Bonnell Street.

Mark hit a dry spot with his right foot and did an amazing wipeout. We must have been going 20-25 miles an hour at that moment. He went down on his right knee like a sack of bricks and then toppled over, landing full force on his right shoulder, and then skidding for another 25 feet on the slick surface. Fortunately no cars were coming the other way.

I dropped off immediately and started running back to Mark. When I reached him, he was lying there flat on his back groaning, "It's my fucking knee, man. I've totaled it!" And then he started crying really hard.

It was his knee. And his ankle. It was also his shoulder. Broken clavicle. And a couple of ribs got badly bruised. He ended up in a wheelchair for two months. He wrote an article for the school paper from his hospital bed, describing in detail what happened and pretty much saying that bumper hitchin' was the coolest thing ever. It fueled the bumper hitchin' craze even more, but the *AP* didn't pick it up.

You couldn't go anywhere that winter without seeing kids waiting for cars to hitch. The local emergency rooms did a booming business.

Reece, however, hung up his bumper hitchin' shoes and moved on to bigger and better things. He learned all the lyrics to the new Hendrix album and began growing the first, and only, Caucasian Afro at our school.

Boys' State

ooney's selection as one of the two delegates to Boys' State from our high school was a foregone conclusion. Mr. Conservative. Straight-laced and grounded like no one else our age. He knew who he was and who he was going to grow up to be. And he was the only one our age with any real interest (bordering on compulsion) in government and politics. His passion was frightening at times.

At Senior Class Night there were a couple of token cheers and catcalls when his name was announced as the first Boys' State delegate representing our school. However, when my name was announced as the second delegate, there was a stunned silence. Disbelief on a gargantuan scale. Then, after reality had set in, that silence was replaced with loud, bellowing laughter and screams. I had to stand and take a bow before they would stop laughing, shouting, and applauding.

That's pretty much the way I saw it, too. A total joke. And I knew whom to blame for this prestigious, life-altering accolade. Turns out that my dad hustled our high school counselor, Mrs. Clifton, the one who made the recommendations to Principal Tucker. He told her that I wanted to be a journalist (true) and that this would be a wonderful chance for me to do some investigative reporting. He even told her that I would be happy (not true) to write a series of pieces for the school paper about the experience. And, last, but not least, he confided in Mrs. Clifton that he had been unable, for health reasons, to attend Boys' State when he was in high school (an out-and-out lie). Counselors never take the time to validate parents' stories. Mrs. Clifton bought it hook, line, and sinker.

In the American Legion literature, Boys' State is described as the place "...for high school upperclassmen to see first-hand what it takes to be leaders in their communities." My read on it was a little different, "an opportunity for high school weirdos to play government dress-up." Most of the delegates saw Boys' State for what it really was—a feather in their cap when applying to the elite colleges. Some also saw it as a chance to meet other weirdoes like themselves. A lot of them even bought the American Legion line about seeing first-hand how our proud democracy functions. Don't get me started.

Booney's reasons for attending Boys' State were rather predictable. First, he said he wanted to see and meet the other attendees. He wanted to learn who they were, what made them tick, and what they were thinking. After all, these were the same guys he would be manipulating on the golf course in years to come. Second, and more importantly, he wanted to note what their strengths and weaknesses were so he could file them away for future use. And third, and most important, he wanted a front-row seat for the Republican Party platform caucus meeting where all the decision making and bill drafting would take place. To secure that seat, he decided, well in advance, to run for Attorney General in the mock election. That way he didn't have to campaign much (he could "ride" the well-established Republican wave) and yet he would still have as much clout as the Governor and Lieutenant Governor. And besides, I'm sure he was the only one attending who had already written bills. He needed to be and would be at the table.

Finn, the other politico in our class (and on the opposite end of the political spectrum from Booney) was only too happy to point out to me that Boys' State was formed in 1935, inspired by the highly popular, Fascist-inspired, Young Pioneer camps. Ah, my story lead! I will owe him for life.

I wasn't surprised when my Boys' State experience started out to be nothing short of boot camp. Up marching around the campus by 6:30 a.m., yelling out our individual dorm floor's (named after the U.S. presidents) war slogan, "Jackson County's the best!" and the brilliant response, "You're right." Then there were the daily chapel services, endless assemblies, nonsensical speeches by delegates, law enforcement speeches by flat-topped guys who looked like Brown Shirts (a hold-over from the Fascist days for sure) and guest speakers including the real Lieutenant Governor.

How I survived the week is beyond me. Fortunately, I knew so little about politics that most of it just seemed like a bad dream. I also learned how to fake the flu (and one 24 hour flare up afterwards) quite successfully.

None of the crap that went on fazed me in the least. I didn't let the forced marches, assemblies, chapel services, and choral sings get to me. They gave me time to think.

Just as he promised, Booney got nominated as Attorney General for the Republican Party. His campaign speech and acceptance speech reeked of old-guard party politics, but he was clever enough to intersperse all the standard crap with pleas for the Republican Party to become the party of our generation. He ended by leading a rousing rendition of "God Bless America" that brought the house down. The *Campus Daily* had his picture on its front page the next morning. The caption read, "Future Leaders Take the Stage." Note: most, if not all, of our future leaders can't keep a tune to save their lives.

On day five, however, things took an unexpected turn. Long after I had retired for the evening with my Jackson County cell mates, Booney was busy hosting a little poker party for some of the big hitters in the Boys' State Republican Party including the Governor, Lieutenant Governor, Secretary of State and his Campaign Strategist, Tom Doble. A calculated gathering to discuss ideas and plot strategy for the big finale on Saturday night, a night Booney hoped would go down in the annals of the American Legion. Cigars, Pepsi, chips, and onion dip. All the major food groups. Five card draw and seven-card stud. Nickel ante. Maybe even a little booze (totally hearsay if you ask me).

According to Booney, one of the less-ambitious (and more jealous) attendees living on the poker floor (who had obviously not been invited) called the Resident Adviser, a university senior with big aspirations, to complain about the noise. Instead of just breaking up the party, the RA called Campus Police to report a major disturbance and possible illegal activity on his floor. Four cop wannabees answered his distress call for help.

Out of nowhere, these four guys, dressed in their university law enforcement finest, came bursting into the room. No guns but otherwise acting like a real, live SWAT team. "OK, it's over! We've called the Boys' State authorities, and the game is up!" Tom was ready with a witty response, "Damn, I had a full house, queens high."

Booney apparently was the only one who laughed. Then, right out of the movies (or one of their training films), one of the cops said, "Oh, a wise guy, huh?" And another cop said, "We want your names, and we want them right now."

This was Booney's cue. "What seems to be the problem, officers?" Their fearless leader replied, "We have received complaints about a loud party going on in this room." And, unable to stop himself, added, "That's what seems to be the problem." Booney decided to just sit back and let them continue to dig their own graves.

After a few more absurd statements by the invaders,

Booney decided to take charge. He told the officers that none of the apparent felons had anything to say and wouldn't until they first talked to American Legion authorities. The cops weren't expecting this (these were high school kids, for God's sake). They were growing more frustrated by the instant. "You're resisting arrest!" Booney, very calmly, said, "We're not resisting anything, and, as far as I know, we haven't been arrested yet."

At a break in the action, Booney told them he had to go to the bathroom and went instead to call me on the hall phone and get me out of bed. He informed me that I had just been appointed (by him) Party Press Secretary and was needed on site immediately to help deal with a very "sensitive matter."

It was too good to be true. I got there in time to witness a classic standoff. The campus cops were "securing the premises" while Booney and his fellow leaders continued to play poker (Tom's idea). Booney introduced me as Communications' Chief (he'd already changed my title) to the head cop and then took me to the card table to get me up-to-speed on what had just transpired. Booney and Tom asked me to record everything said from then on. It was truly an out-of-body experience.

Within the half hour, one of the Grand Poobahs from the American Legion showed up and began damage control. I have no idea who called him. And, after forty-five minutes of comical banter, a compromise was reached between the him and the cops. There was lots of backslapping. No charges would be filed, and we would stop playing cards. By this time the Campus

Police Supervisor was present too, so we had a real "meeting of the minds." And I got it all down on paper!

I went back to my dorm and did what any professional Communications' Chief would do. I called the local and state papers and leaked the story. To the *Free Press,* I remained anonymous but told them about the potentially violent encounter that had just occurred. To the local paper, I identified myself, complete with Party title, and gave them some juicy quotes. It was a gas. Booney came across as the champion of the common man. In the process of covering the story, the *Free Press* uncovered the fact that our Boys' State Lieutenant Governor, present in the room, was the stepson of the former Governor of Michigan. His parents came and took him home. The next afternoon the former Governor was quoted as saying his son no longer planned to attend the host institution in the fall.

Booney, Tom, and I pretty much took over the Republican Party the night of the "bust." We orchestrated and ran the election campaign, winning all the major offices except Lieutenant Governor. By that time we had written the closing speech for the Saturday night rally and told the other Republican nominees that Booney would be delivering it, not the Governor-elect. No one complained.

Booney really nailed the speech. It was short and sweet but packed full of juicy tidbits and sappy one-liners. Our theme was security and our intent was to compare and contrast our nation's Cold War posture with local enforcement security issues. Considering I didn't believe any of the content, I think it's the best writing I did in high school by a long shot.

"My friends, you and I must feel safe in our own communities. We must be able to rely on our law enforcement officials to protect us and yet also not infringe on our God-given rights so aptly set down by our forefathers in the Bill of Rights." And Booney delivered it like he was standing in the pulpit on Sunday morning.

I wrote only one Boys' State article for the school paper. I gave Booney high marks and won him enormous respect from the YAF state chapter. I wasn't quite so positive about my Boys' State experience. Perhaps my first sentence partially explains why our paper's teacher adviser was replaced soon after the article appeared. "Rick Boone and I attended Boys' State for a week this past summer and came face-to-face with the American Legion's answer to the 1930's Fascist's Young Pioneer Camps." Good, solid journalism if you ask me.

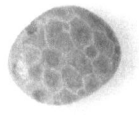

In My Room

I didn't sleep again. Even the rain didn't help. This makes four nights in a row. I've read the latest *Sports Illustrated* four times cover to cover. I've relived every race I ever ran and every touchdown I ever scored and should have scored.

I'm a prisoner in my own room. In the last week I've studied every inch of this space. The baseball wallpaper with hats from all the teams, the twin beds with the baseball comforters, the windows and the window seat under the south-facing window, my desk and all my books, model airplanes and battleships, my bulletin board with all the sports' clippings, my medals, my reel-to-reel tape recorder, my radio, my closet, the light above my bed, the baseball lamp on the night stand between the beds, and all the pictures of me, my family, and my friends. (Funny thing. I didn't play baseball in high school and yet my whole bedroom is baseball.)

I just went downstairs to be around Mom and Dad for a while. It didn't work. Mom wanted to know why I wasn't out with "the other boys" or over at Debby's house. "You aren't going to see her until Thanksgiving!"

All I could think to say was, "I have to pack." Then Mom said, "We're going to miss you terribly, Darling," speaking for both of them. I heard Mom say to Dad as I was going back upstairs, "I don't know what he's talking about. He's been packed for over a week." Dad added, "Did you notice he hasn't showered or even combed his hair? I wonder if he and Debby broke up." And Mom responded coldly and matter-of-factly, "I'd know if they had. They're fine." End of conversation. This is her world. Dad and I are threatening it.

I should talk to someone about this. If I told Mom, she wouldn't believe me. No, that's not it. She wouldn't let herself believe it. She'd just say I was imagining the whole thing...that I can do anything I set my mind to do. Dad would act like it was all in my head and, if I was strong enough, I could beat it. He might even say those immortal familial words, "Snap out of it. You're a Thompson, aren't you?"

Maybe I should just tell everyone I'm not going. They'd all be really pissed and disappointed, but they'd get over it sooner or later. Maybe.

Shit. WLAV just played "In My Room" by the Beach Boys. It's gotta be a sign. "There's a world where I can go and tell my secrets to. In my room."

What's amazing about all this is that no one really knows anything about me. Everyone has their preconceived notions of who I am...All-American boy, good athlete, good student, very popular, natural leader, easy to be with, friendly. Up until now, all that fit me pretty well. Not any longer. It's a whole different ballgame. Why does it all have to change? Why can't everything stay the way it was before graduation? I'm not ready for it to change. I may never be ready.

My friends can't wait to get to college and leave high school behind. They talk about doing new things, making new friends, seeing new places. Are any of them faking it? Could one of them be as scared as I am? How can I find out without letting them know what's going on with me? I've never been afraid of anything in my life. This isn't supposed to happen to me.

This is fear of the unknown, that's what it is. I have no control over it. I think I'm about to have a nervous breakdown. Hell, I think I'm in the middle of one right now.

It's time for a pep talk. Just like the ones I used to give myself before a big calculus test, football game, or track meet. Pretty much what Mom and Dad said to me downstairs, "How badly do you want it? No one can touch you and you know it. Show them what you've got. You can do this."

I can do this. I have to do this. I hope I can do this. I've gotta get some sleep.

I can't do this. What the fuck am I going to do?

Big Dog on Campus

"Taking a nap?"

Without opening my eyes, I responded, "Not any more."

"Whoa. A little testy, wouldn't you say?"

I opened my eyes. I was lying on the quad grass on campus. Beautiful fall day. Most of the other students were in class. I was making a rebellious stand. I'm a writer and don't need to be in school to practice my trade. I get my inspiration from naps like this.

A black Labrador was staring down at me, with a goofy puppy smirk on his face. Frisbee in his mouth and no one else around. I jumped straight up.

"Holy shit, man," I said. "What the fuck are you doing?"

"Interesting response," said the lab. "You're the one talking to a dog."

"Give me a break. I was sound asleep for Christ's sake."

"Drugs, right?"

"Nope. Maybe nothing surprises me anymore."

The dog continued his line of interrogation. "So what's your thing?"

"Right now I'm writing a book."

"Oh yeah. I've heard about you. Are you the quiet one? Or the brainaholic? A guy throwing for me the other day said something about one of you guys. What was it? Oh yeah. You are a conceited, stuck-up prick."

"That's the brainaholic. I must be the quiet one. So what's your thing?"

"Amazing. You just jump right into a conversation with a dog. Well, because we're being completely honest with each other, excuse me for just a second while I bark a laugh or two. Speaking of which, I'll bet you didn't know that a lot of our barks are really laughs. No charge for that little tidbit." He barked and then continued answering my question.

"Ah, much better. Well, you're my mark right now. Gotta stay in shape. And you looked liked a good challenge. You know, can I get this passed out guy to throw me a couple? You like dogs?"

"Sure. But it's probably not a good time for me to have one."

"I'm not looking for housing at the present time. Let me guess. You grew up with a cocker spaniel, right?"

"You're good. Great dog, too."

"Why don't you write a story about a dog? Me for instance."

"What's the hook?" I was talking literature with a dog.

"Well, it could be a shaggy dog thing. College kid talking to a dog. Then the two of them do something crazy. Fred McMurray kind of thing, you know?"

"No one would believe it."

"Even better."

"Do you live around here?"

He barked out a couple more laughs, much louder this time.

"Sorry, your questions crack me up. Well, right now I'm living with a nice faculty couple. We've got a good arrangement. They know I'll bolt if they lock me up all day. So they're cool with me hanging out on campus during the day and then going 'home' at night (he raised his right paw in quotes) to flop by the fireplace and help create that perfect family feeling, minus kids."

"Very touching. What's your name?"

"You're too much, man. Take your pick."

"What do your new owners call you?"

"Promise you won't laugh? Mayall...as in John Mayall."

I couldn't help it. I laughed.

"Fuck you."

"I haven't seen you here before."

"Very observant. Just got into town. Scouted out the potential adoptees and this couple just fell into my lap. Turns out he just took a job here at the college and is a tad lonely. We were meant for each other."

"Do you talk to them?"

"Come on. Are you kidding? They'd think I was a freak and get rid of me."

"So am I the only one that you talk to?"

"You got that right." Mayall flopped over on the ground and kicked up his legs into the sky. "Scratch my belly. Pretend for a second that this is just a dog and his new buddy kind of thing."

I did as he suggested. Mayall continued talking while

rolling on his back. "He and his wife really love me. I fill a void in their lives. They need me, and I'm cool with that."

"You're going to make me cry."

"You've got a good sense of humor. Joking with a dog. Come on, humor me some more. Throw me one. Long. Watch me do my thing. I promise you won't be disappointed. Ride my innate talent to a little instant fame."

Mayall dropped the frisbee on the ground beside me and took off running. I picked it up and threw it. Best frisbee throw I've ever made. Long and straight. And sure enough, Mayall ran under it, leapt way up in the air and caught it. Several students reacted. A couple of whistles. A few claps. We were instant stars.

A guy I didn't know came up to me. He was eating a big cupcake.

"Great dog. How did you teach him to do that?"

"He's a natural. Hey, could you spare a piece of that cupcake? He's been out doing this for the last half hour and is running a little low on fuel."

Mayall had come trotting back, basking in the glory. He dropped the frisbee on the ground in front of me.

"Mayall, this nice man has a bite of cupcake for you."

"Great name, man."

"Thanks. It fits him pretty well. There's no one like him."

Mayall spoke but, thankfully, I was the only one able to hear him.

"You learn fast." And he chuckled. "Tell me to sit and

roll over in both directions."

I did, and Mayall put on quite a show. He bounced back up, came to a sitting position and gingerly took his piece of cupcake. Then I threw him another frisbee, and he made an equally great catch.

The guy had been joined by three other fans, and they were all blown away. One said, "You should train dogs for a living. You'd make a million."

Mayall just took it in stride. So did I.

Then Mayall yelped like someone had stepped on him by mistake. "Shit, here comes my owner."

I turned and saw Dr. Warner of the English Department coming our way. He called Mayall, and Mayall hopped to it. Faithful pet. I followed after him.

Warner looked a little defensive. "That's my dog."

"You're lucky. He's a great athlete."

"I think he's losing a step or two though."

Mayall said, "He's full of shit. "

I laughed out loud, and Warner gave me a look. I interjected in Mayall's defense, "Maybe, but he's really smart."

Mayall couldn't stand it any more. "Do me a favor?"

I didn't react in front of Warner. Mayall glared at me. "Please. Pretty please. I'll owe you."

Under my breath, pretending to clear my throat, I bent over and said to him, "What could you possibly…"

Mayall cut me off. "Think about it. Great way to meet chicks, right?"

I repeated the throat clearing exercise, "OK. What?"

"Ask him how his textbook is coming. No one knows

about it. It'll freak him out."

"How's your textbook coming, Dr. Warner?"

Warner looked at me in total shock. "Excuse me?"

"How's the writing coming?"

"How could you possibly know that I was working on a textbook?"

Mayall laughed. "Improvise."

"I'm a writer, too. I can just sense these things."

Warner challenged me, "Who told you?"

"Your dog."

"Jesus Christ." Then he laughed out loud in relief and started walking back toward the Fine Arts' Building.

I called out after him, "Nice to meet you. My name's Tim."

He responded in a condescending tone, "So it is. So it is."

Mayall was beside himself. "What the fuck was that? Hey, I've got an idea. Run and catch up with him. Tell him you'd be happy to take me for walks during the day."

And that's exactly what I did. Warner bit. "That would be great. He needs the exercise and it'd be safer. Right now, we just let him out in the morning and hope he comes back. Stop by my office tomorrow around 4 p.m. and we'll talk more about this. Of course, I insist on paying you."

I smiled. "And I insist on accepting."

Warner's body language changed in a flash from dog owner to professor again, and off he walked, already deep in thought.

"She's pregnant," Mayall said. "They don't know

it yet, but I do. And I know what that means for me. I'm going to have to split. They're going to have their hands full. No time for a dog."

I didn't know what to say. I was thinking I should retract my earlier statement about this not being a good time to have a dog.

Mayall interrupted my thought. "It's OK. You don't have to do that. I want to see the country. You know, like the guy on the tv show? Bronson, isn't it?"

He picked up his frisbee and started prancing off in search of his next thrower. He spun around and, out of the corner of his mouth said, "Catch you later. Get it?" And then he barked a couple of good laughs. "Hey, someone really needs to get a water bowl out here for all us dogs that hang out on the quad."

"I'll get right on it, Mayall. See you around."

Not concerned by what others might hear or think, I barked back at him. I have no idea what I said. And off I went to fetch a water bowl.

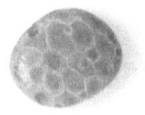

Listen to This!

"You got a second?"

I was on the way to the campus library to study and sleep, not necessarily in that order. This older guy, standing out on the front porch of a two-story dive, was pointing at me. "I need your help."

He seemed harmless. Wearing a Cubs' hat. Stroh's can in his right hand. So I walked up the steps toward him. "Do a good deed" time, I thought.

Beaming from ear to ear, he bellowed, "Come on in here and sit down."

I did as he said, never questioning the sanity of my decision.

He walked in ahead of me not bothering to hold the door. The house smelled of mold and stale beer. The living room walls were peeling badly. He had cut up a carpet into several smaller, irregular "rugs" and randomly tossed them around the room.

I'd seen him somewhere before. I just couldn't remember where. Most likely somewhere on campus.

He pointed silently in the direction of a ratty looking upholstered chair. I went and sat down, very carefully, realizing what clean freaks must go through every day.

He headed to his ancient record player, a man on a mission. Without looking up from the record he'd chosen, he barked, "I want you to listen to this song." And then, in a damn good boot camp impersonation, "And I mean listen and listen good."

His demanding, booming tone was totally unexpected and uncalled for. After all, I was doing him a favor! Right?

The song began. I immediately recognized the tune. "Glen Campbell. 'Gentle On My Mind,'" I said.

He flipped around to face me and whispered as loudly as he dared whisper and still be able to hear the song. "Shut up. That's not important. Listen, for God's sake."

After another 30 seconds, he leapt out of his chair and began pacing back and forth, doing very pronounced spin turns at the walls. Like a bear confined in his cage.

Clearly I had made a serious error in judgment.

Glen sang on, "By the rivers of my memory that keeps you ever gentle on my mind."

The song finished, and the guy weighed in immediately, "That just kills me. John Hartford wrote that, you know."

"I guess I didn't know that. Thanks so much for sharing your song with me." I stood up to leave, but he stepped in front of me and effortlessly blocked my way.

"He and Glen both won Grammies for it."

I was getting more uncomfortable by the second. "I didn't know that either."

"I'm not through with you yet. You haven't told me what you think of the song."

I just blurted it out. "It's a haunting love story, that's

what it is. Should we pity him? He's a bum after all. But is that even relevant? No, I would contend. He is part of the human condition. He has his memories. They are with him everywhere he goes, and she is very real in his mind, fictitious or not. And that makes him very lucky. It brings meaning to his horrible life. We should all be that lucky."

He went ballistic. "Holy shit! You get it. God damn it, you get it! You do understand." He was jumping up and down for joy like a little kid. This guy was totally off his rocker. "I knew you'd understand. There was no one else I could trust. And now the door has been opened and the secret revealed. You have aced the test of all tests."

That's when I exploded out the door and jumped off the steps to freedom before he could even react.

Now he was screaming at me. "You call yourself a lover of music? A connoisseur of the finer things in life? Passionate about the mysteries of the universe? Why are you leaving? You've seen the light. You must stay and celebrate this marvelous moment in music history!"

And then I remembered where I'd seen him before. He was a janitor in the Biology Building on campus. He hummed tunes all the time at work. He must have recognized me.

I walked a few steps back toward him. I'm too nice a guy. I remembered his name as I walked up to him. "Tony, are you ok?"

"What the hell does that mean? Am I OK? What's OK? Who's OK? What's the standard for OK? Who decides who's OK and who isn't?" And he erupted into a crazy laugh.

"Hey, I just asked you if you're OK, Tony."

"So you do remember me?"

"I do."

"There are others, you know."

"Others?'

"Other songs waiting to be unlocked. Just like "Gentle On My Mind." Screaming for their moment in the sun."

I wasn't going back inside that house.

As I turned to leave again, I heard laughter coming from inside the house. Laughter I recognized. And the coin dropped. I'd been set up. My sometime roommate (and full-time asshole), Duke, came outside and stood behind Tony, putting his arms around him.

"Holy shit. You fell for it! Absolutely amazing."

"You're a prick, Duke."

"Yeah, I deserve that, but it's been well worth it. A job well done all the way around. My idea, Tony's masterful acting performance, and your totally insane response. Too fucking incredible. Analyzing a Glen Campbell song. No one will believe this."

I was ready. "You're wrong about that. It's a hell of a song, and I meant everything I said. The lyrics are heavy – powerful and thought provoking."

I began reciting:

> "It's knowing that your door is always open
> And your path is free to walk
> That makes me tend to leave my sleeping bag
> Rolled up and stashed behind your couch

And it's knowing I'm not shackled
By forgotten words and bonds
And the ink stains that have dried upon some
line
That keeps you in the backroads
By the rivers of my mem'ry
That keeps you ever gentle on my mind."

I glanced at Tony. He didn't look so good. His eyes were darting back and forth, and I wasn't so sure he was on the same wavelength as Duke.

I was on a roll now. "I'm sorry the two of you can't appreciate that. Your loss. You have offended one of the great lyricists of our time, and you should both be ashamed of yourselves." And I walked off to the sound of Duke's clapping.

I'd gotten about ten steps when I heard Tony scream out, " Ask the Smother's Brothers. Ask the Byrds. John Hartford is a genius."

I turned to see him running toward me, yelling and jumping like a total nut case. When he caught up to me, he grabbed me, gave me a huge bear hug, and said in my ear, "Let's see how Duke handles this little twist in the program." And off he went, screaming even louder.

Now Duke was running toward me yelling, "You've got to help me! I fucked up, man. Tony's lost it. He's going to do something crazy. We've got to stop him!"

Thirty yards down the block, Tony suddenly stopped and turned to face us. "How do you like it now, Duke?"

Paris Peace Talks

I n retrospect, this was a meeting long overdue, and it all came to a head last night. Actually about 3 a.m. I woke up and couldn't get back to sleep (which is pretty rare for me). So I went out to the kitchen for a glass of water, knowing full well that when I turned on the light, cockroaches would scurry in all directions as fast as their six legs could carry them.

That's not what happened. I turned on the light, but the roaches (and I'm thinking there were 20-25 of them scattered across several locations in the room) stood firm. It was quickly apparent that they were all staring at me. I panned the room to see if I could recognize a leader. No one stood out.

I walked over to the sink very carefully, not wanting to step on one by accident.

Something wasn't right. You could cut the tension – all that insect adrenaline – with a knife. I got a glass of water and sat down at the kitchen table. Four of the larger roaches, gathered on the left front stove burner, moved to the middle of the stove and turned to face me. One of them spoke. I guess I was relieved.

"I don't believe we've seen you here at this time of night. We see the other two all the time but not you."

I had to explain to a cockroach this aberration in my sleep behavior? "I couldn't sleep. I was thirsty so I got up to get a drink." And then, for some unknown reason I added, "Got a problem with that?" Simultaneously I thought, great, now I'm antagonizing a bunch of cockroaches.

The smallest of the foursome, glancing at his three companions, responded, "Well actually, come to think of it, we do."

It was like I was a different person. I was uncharacteristically provoking the situation, "And that would be?"

"We're tired of being interrupted in the middle of the night while we're eating. This is our time."

I came to my senses. There was nothing to be gained by pissing them off. I tried to change to a friendlier tone, "I have no problem with that." Though in the back of my mind, I was beginning to hope this was a dream.

"We know who you are," said another roach who had just climbed up onto the table within a foot of me. "Your roommates talk about you."

"Really. What do they say?"

"It's not appropriate for us to comment on that."

I was suddenly talking to these roaches like they were my best buddies.

"Oh, come on. What the fuck does that mean?"

That's all it took. The little one spoke again, "The two of them are frequently here together about this time. Eating for the most part. But they do exchange some information. I'll tell you what, you're the only one in this house getting anything done."

There was a part of me that had the same feeling.

Another roach, on the floor by the back door, got up his nerve and spoke, "You don't seem to be repulsed by us in the least."

"Nope. Biology major. According to my professors, your species has been on this planet a lot longer than ours. And, it's probably safe to say that you'll be here long after ours is gone."

The first roach responded, "Well put. We concur." Another roach, who sounded like an excited kid, spewed forth supporting data. "Yeah, we've been here several hundred million years. I've got a question for you. True or false. The name cockroach comes from the Spanish word, cucaracha."

I bit. "I say false."

He flipped his antennae up and down. "And you would be wrong, Mr. Know-It-All!"

The sound of roach clicking filled the room. Roach laughter without a doubt.

The roach who had spoken first continued, "So, can we begin negotiations?"

"What negotiations?"

Ignoring my question, he continued. "Let me begin by saying that it is our intent to craft a meaningful and acceptable settlement for both our parties. To that end, we promise to bargain in good faith."

More clicking but this time it wasn't laughter. They were obviously serious now. I heard myself say, "Fine.

I can't speak for my roommates, but I will certainly convey the specifics of this negotiation process to them and get back to you."

He detected the tone in my voice. "I'm trying to establish a cooperative tone here. We feel this is the perfect time to initiate talks that will conclude with a suitable outcome for both parties. And we believe that you are the proper one to represent the position of you and your roommates."

I couldn't help but laugh. "Well, you have to admit this doesn't happen every day. I'm trying to imagine how my roommates will react to this. They'll probably tell me to back way off on the hash. They may go so far as to demand that I stop reading Carlos Castaneda."

He continued, "We must be serious if we hope to reconcile our differences. I might suggest at this juncture that you consider the bigger picture. What happens here will be analyzed by experts of all species for years to come."

The budding biologist in me kicked in, "Don't you guys only live for a year?"

"These negotiations are for the next generations."

"Any other concerns before we begin?," a judicial-sounding roach said.

"Actually I have two other questions. Will this agreement be with your group or all the roaches who live in this area?"

"Good question. There are four and some say five other species in this state, but we are the only species you will ever see in your house. *Blattella germanica.*

That's us. And this agreement will be between our group who lives here now and you three."

"So what's to stop another group of your species from moving in? Would we have to do another agreement with them?"

Now he began counseling me, "You're getting unnecessarily worked up."

Probably right, but I was on a roll. "Isn't it true that, if we cleaned our apartment at all, you wouldn't be here, and these talks would be unnecessary?"

"We doubt seriously, knowing your roommates, that that would ever happen."

And so it began. The negotiation process brought new meaning to the phrase "coming to the table." The table in this instance was the kitchen table. Four cockroaches and I. The others gathered in a circle, but at a distance in case negotiations broke down and things turned nasty.

The little guy made the first demand. "We want exclusive access to the kitchen from 2 to 6 a.m."

"That won't work. Bart and Tucker don't go to bed until at least 3 a.m. How about 3 to 7 a.m? I'm the first one up, as you obviously know, but I can refrain from coming into the kitchen until 7."

The roaches at the table looked at one another and all nodded. The little guy responded, "That sounds agreeable. And that's the extent of our needs. We'll give you 48 hours to talk with your roommates and get back to us. If we haven't heard by then, we plan to move into the living room. And after that we'll move into the bedrooms."

"That sounds pretty militaristic to me."

"We know humans respond better to threats than to pacifistic pleas. Gandhi was the exception to the rule."

It was my turn. "What do we get in return?"

The clicking started again. The little guy was doing all the talking for them now. "What do you want?"

"We don't see any of you from 6 to 10 pm"

After another half minute or so of clicking, he turned to me and said, "That's a fair request."

"So how the hell do you suggest I get my roommates to listen to me, let alone take me seriously?"

He was ready with an answer, "We have confidence in you and believe that you'll find a way to talk to them. Personally, I would suggest you tell them the bedrooms are fair game if matters can't be resolved quickly."

Then, another roach who had not spoken until now, said, "One of your roommates hates us, and the other one appears to be terrified of us. I would suggest that a small group of us join you when you discuss these proposals with them."

This idea was clearly controversial. There were two distinct clicking sounds coming from the perimeter that I took to be strong disagreement and guarded agreement.

And then, in a well-rehearsed medley, two of the smaller (perhaps younger) roaches decided it was a good time to take turns reciting quotes they'd committed to memory.

"War doesn't determine who is right, only who is left. Bertrand Russell."

"What's more immoral than war? Marquis de Sade."

"Sometime they'll give a war and no one will come. Carl Sandburg."

"I destroy my enemies when I make them my friends. Abraham Lincoln."

"There never was a good war or a bad peace. Benjamin Franklin."

"The basic problems facing the world today are not susceptible to a military solution. John F. Kennedy."

"An eye for an eye makes the whole world blind. Mahatma Gandhi."

"We have guided missiles and misguided men. Martin Luther King, Jr."

I hadn't expected the quotes. "Very impressive."

One of them responded quickly, "We've been waiting a long time to do that."

"Glad I could help."

The little guy at the table continued, "Well, a majority supports our colleague's suggestion to have a small team of us present to assist you with your presentation."

By now, that sounded quite reasonable to me. "Hey, it's worth a try. I'll talk to them tonight. In the best of all worlds, they'll both be stoned and in a better frame of mind to deal with this."

And with that, we said our goodbyes. I went back to bed and dreamed of talking to cockroaches about politics and sports.

The next night was pretty predictable. My room-mates were both stoned, listening to music and looking at magazines in the living room. I walked in, turned off the turntable and proceeded to tell them that I had had a meeting with the roaches in our apartment the night before. Shortly after I finished explaining to them what the roaches had proposed and how I had countered, four of the roaches climbed up on the ottoman beside me, and looked right at Bart and Tucker. I couldn't introduce them since I didn't know their names, but I did nod to the four of them and then said to Bart and Tucker, "These are a few of the roaches I talked to last night. They asked if they could be here tonight to corroborate our conversation."

Bart, the one who didn't like roaches, got up and quietly walked out of the room shaking his head. Tucker just sat there frozen. He couldn't believe what he was seeing and was incapable of speaking. He just stared at them for what seemed to be three or four minutes, occasionally looking at me as if to say, "What the fuck is going on? Do you know how bad this looks? Do you realize how utterly absurd this is?"

Finally, he stood up and left the room, too. One of the roaches commented. "Gee, that went well. We should do it again some time real soon." And off they went.

The bad news first. The next day Bart announced he was moving out and asked Tucker if he wanted to join him. Tucker said yes, so, by 5 pm, they were both gone.

The good news is that I got two new roommates, both biology majors. And I never had to have another negotiating session with the roaches. Biology majors go to bed early.

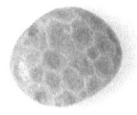

Day of Firsts

"Are you all right?"

I jerked awake and saw this woman standing over me. I quickly looked around to get my bearings. I was on the bench out in front of the post office downtown.

"I've been shopping for over an hour. You were here when I arrived, and you're still here."

"I'm fine. I guess I just fell asleep."

"Are you a student at the college?"

"Yes. Well, normally."

"Did something happen?"

"No, nothing happened. It's just a little confusing, that's all."

"Try me."

"I'm enrolled but I'm having serious second thoughts about school and the United States for that matter."

She was being extremely forward, and I had no idea why. I found myself studying her. Something I don't do as a general rule. 30ish. Wedding ring. Pretty. Dark, curly hair. Good looking. Hell, gorgeous. Maybe a professor's wife. I definitely didn't get a "townie" vibe.

Balancing three shopping bags as well as a hippie-type shoulder bag. Dressed down with dark corduroys and a faded purple sweater.

"How about you?" (It just came out of my mouth.)

"Me?"

I heard myself repeat her line. "Try me."

"I just saw you here, thought it was odd, or interesting, and decided to come over."

She stopped, looked around, and said, "I deserved that. I was just concerned. You don't look like the park bench type."

"But I do love this bench." And then another out-of-body line. "Want to join me? I guarantee it's the most comfortable bench in the county."

She didn't hesitate. She sat down on the bench and put her bags down beside her.

"Sounds like you've been doing a lot of research."

"I'm going out on a limb actually. I've really only tested five or six, but this one is by far the best."

She moved around a bit as if to test the bench out.

"I see what you mean."

"You strike me as the trusting type."

"I don't believe I've ever been accused of that before."

"Well, today's a day of firsts then."

"Name one of your firsts."

"I've never had anyone speak to me while I was sitting on this bench."

"I've never spoken to anyone on this bench before."

She turned to face me head-on. "I've never been this forward before with someone I don't know."

"Me neither."

"I'm sorry."

"Me, too."

"For what?"

"For whatever you're sorry for."

We didn't say anything for a minute or so. People were walking by, but I was no longer paying any attention. I turned to her. "You get two questions, and so do I."

"Excuse me?"

"Flip you to see who goes first."

Without skipping a beat, she reached into her purse and took out a quarter and handed it to me.

"Call it in the air."

"Heads."

I threw it up in the air, caught it, and flipped it over.

"Heads it is. You go first then."

"No, that means I get first choice. And I choose you go first."

"Honest answers?"

"Fair enough."

We sat there quietly again for a minute or so. A harried mother scurried by us with two devilish-looking kids pulling her in opposite directions. She visibly glared at my seat mate.

"Tell me five things about yourself."

She burst into laughter.

"What's so funny?"

"I thought you were going to ask me if I was playing the role of Mrs. Robinson in today's episode."

She was quiet for another minute. A guy I vaguely knew walked by and gave me a look that said, "You lucky son of a bitch."

Then I heard her voice. "OK, here goes.

> *Number one:* I love to read. No. I want to rephrase that. I love to escape in books.
>
> *Number two:* I keep a diary in my head. I've already started this entry.
>
> *Number three:* I miss my sister horribly. She died four years ago in a car crash. It wasn't her fault.
>
> *Number four:* I'm happily married with three children.
>
> *Number five:* I like benches, too."

"Wow. That was incredible."

"Alright, my turn. Describe your girlfriend."

"She's 35ish. Medium height. Curly, dark hair. Radiant looks. She likes to wear bold colors like purple and deep brown. Full of ideas and wonder. Incredibly passionate. I've never met anyone like her before in my life."

"I asked for that."

"You can have another turn." I wanted this to go on forever.

"Tell me five things about yourself."

Three of the five came to me right away so I just started, hoping the other two would surface soon.

> "*Number one:* My dad died a month ago, and I was totally unprepared for it.
>
> *Number two:* I sit here a lot just to think and to

watch people go by.

Number three: You're the most beautiful woman I've ever talked to in my life."

The other two just slipped out.

"*Number four:* I haven't been to a class in over a week, but I think I'm ready to return now.

Number five: I don't need a diary. I will never forget this moment."

She didn't say anything. My mind was racing. It was my turn to ask a question. Don't fuck up by asking a yes or no question. Make sure it's open-ended. Some possibilities popped into my mind. Would you tell me about yourself when you were my age? Or, if you could live anywhere in the world, where would it be?

Then I heard myself say, "Do you play the piano?"

She gasped.

"I haven't played in years. No, that's not right. I enjoy playing piano but haven't had a chance to for many years."

She was more beautiful than any woman I'd ever seen in my life. She was both strong and vulnerable.

Then I heard her say, "Would you kiss me?"

We kissed. It was just incredible. She closed her eyes. I didn't. I just stared at her. I couldn't believe this was happening. Her lips were soft with intent. Not that I had enough experience to know what that meant. My lips were stiff on contact but immediately fell under her lips' spell.

She opened her eyes. They were damp. She touched

her right index finger to my lips. I kissed it. Then, she stood up, picked up her bags, and started to walk away.

"Bye," she said. "Peace." She made the peace sign with her right hand.

I was in shock. "Wait. What about your second question?"

She turned around as if she'd forgotten something and said simply, "I already asked it."

I wanted to yell something like, "Please ask me another. Hell, ask me as many questions as you want. Take me away with you."

She turned away and kept walking. She never looked back. I watched her cross the street, get into her car, back out of her parking spot, and drive off.

What I wanted more than anything in the whole world was to get in that car with her and just drive away. At that moment I would have traded everything for that.

I slumped down in the bench. I was mentally and physically exhausted. Starting my own diary in my head.

Open Wide

It was something we just didn't talk about. Not surprising really. Mom sure as hell wasn't going to talk about it. She has terrible teeth. Of course, you'd never know. I didn't know for a long time. She has a bright, full smile that gives no hint of the rampant caries lurking within her genetically compromised mouth.

There were distinct clues, however. First, she never scheduled her dental "visits" (her word choice, plural intended) at the same time she scheduled mine. And when she came home, we (Dad, my brother and I) always went out to dinner. She stayed at home to "rest." Second, she always sat in the waiting room as close to the door as she could (probably in case she decided to make a run for it). Third, when I went for one of my visits (referred to as a "cleaning" by our dentist), and the dentist would say, "Mother, could you come in here for just a minute?," Mom would come in, looking like she was about to die. And she never looked at what the dentist wanted to show her.

Our dentist, Dr. Amato, wore really thick glasses. Not very reassuring. It made me wonder if he practiced dentistry by feel. His other most distinctive features: prolific ear and nose hair (much more than he had on the top of his head), an annoying laugh, and really bad breath. I think he ate garlic salami for breakfast. He also hummed to himself all the time (so he wouldn't have to talk to his patients is my guess) but couldn't come close to keeping a tune. And he hummed the same song every time I was there.

His secretary, Grace, doubled as dental assistant, neither happily nor competently. So, if you saw her coming into the room, it was time to go on high alert. When she peered in my mouth (more like squinting when you only want to partially watch a scary movie), I saw total fear and disgust. Her face certainly did not inspire confidence or security. It said "run, save yourself, or otherwise your blood will be scattered over this entire room!"

Then there was the dental equipment. Because Dr. Amato didn't want to talk, and Grace was too terrified and nauseated to, I never knew what the various instruments and machines did. The polishing machine was the scariest of them all. Its different sounds terrified me. I was convinced it was the tool used to rate the value of each tooth, what could stay, and what would have to be pulled or totally covered with fillings.

When we left after my cleanings, Mom wouldn't say anything. I mean, what was she going to say? "Your mouth will now hurt for weeks. You'll end up losing most of your teeth before you're 30. And the ones that are left will look like hell and hurt all the time, but smile, Honey, you're still alive. Just look at me."

I think Dad talked to her about the way she handled these visits, because one time she spoke those immortal words, "Let's go get some ice cream, Darling. You've earned it." Now, I'm the ultimate ice cream addict. And yet that day I heard myself say, in an out-of-body voice, "No thanks, Mom. I think I prefer to just go home and collapse."

The summer after my freshman year of college, I learned I had to have my lower wisdom teeth removed. At one point, Mom even said, "You've grown up so fast. Here comes another rite of passage for you." Thanks to her, I'm sure both my teeth were growing in horizontally.

Grace was still there and greeted me when I walked into the office. She'd never done that before. Something was up. Something wasn't right. She looked relaxed. Her desktop was immaculate, she was smiling, and there were fresh flowers on the little table beside her desk. And she was wearing a colorful mini-skirt. Maybe she really got off on extreme pain and had dressed for this special occasion.

I was wrong. So wrong. And it didn't take long to see why she was so happy. The new dental assistant, Thomas Becker, came bounding into the waiting room. Sticking out his right hand and giving me a powerful handshake and a pat on the back, Thomas boomed out, "You must be Timothy!"

"Tim."

"Well, today's the big day. How are you feeling?"

I wanted to say scared to shit. I wanted to scream, "How the fuck do you think I feel? I'm having two teeth removed, I got my mom's genes for shitty teeth and who knows what else, and this is the worst day of my life. And what the fuck do you care? And, oh yeah, I didn't sleep at all last night after I had this nightmare that all my lower teeth had fallen out. Does that answer your god dam question, you sadistic son-of-a-bitch?"

But I didn't. Thomas was either a total joke or the real McCoy. I chose to go with the latter. I was in survival mode. He really did seem excited. He exuded confidence and caring.

"If Grace has finished all your paperwork," he began.

Grace stepped on his line and chirped out prettily, "Oh Thomas, of course I have. You know that!" And then she visibly blushed and giggled. She was in love with Thomas. Not only was he a hunk (you could see it in her eyes), he was the brave knight who had come to save her from her former second job as dental assistant.

Thomas winked at Grace and continued. "Tim (he had actually listened!), do you have someone to drive you home after today's procedure?"

Resisting the temptation to say, "Yes, Reynolds and Biteoff Funeral Home will be handling my body today," I responded, "My dad will be here soon." Of course, my mom wasn't coming within ten miles of this place today. The guilt was far too overpowering. She had probably taken to her bed in anticipation of my dad's phone call from the Emergency Room at the hospital ("Dotty, there's been a horrible accident at Dr. Amato's.").

Into the examination office we went – my new best friend, Thomas, and I. And there was Looney (that's what I secretly called Dr. Amato), looking out the window and humming to the actual song playing on the stereo. Stop right there. Stereo? That's right, there was a really nice record player and reel-to-reel tape deck on the counter that had previously held Looney's old dental school textbooks. Speakers were mounted on all four of the corner walls. No more radio oozing out instrumental crap. Instead I was hearing the chorus of "Grazin' in the Grass," the Friends of Distinction's vocal cover of the Hugh Masekela hit instrumental. When Looney turned around, singing along ("Can you dig it, can you dig it baby!"), I was totally shocked. He was wearing a bold short sleeve, madras shirt, wire rimmed glasses (still incredibly thick but very hip), bell-bottom jeans, and sandals. His hair was much longer, his nose and ear hair trimmed, and he had a bushy moustache. And he was singing in tune.

Walking over to the turntable he said, "Tim, how's it goin'?"

"Great," I heard myself say. I should have been anything but great, but there I was, smiling at the man who would soon tear my mouth apart. He had actually spoken to me!

"Well, first things first. Would you be so kind as to join me over here?" Directing me to the record counter. I walked over there timidly. Was this a trick? He continued. "What would you like to listen to while Thomas and I do our magic?"

Unbelievable. I was now staring at a record collection that any kid my age would kill for. He had the Temptations, Beatles, Beach Boys, Fifth Dimension, Sly, Marvin Gaye, Creedence, Junior Walker, the Stones, Animals, Blood, Sweat and Tears, the Grass Roots, the Guess Who, the Rascals, Four Tops, Classics IV, Nilsson, the Lovin' Spoonful. Hell, he had everyone. And there it was. My album. I picked it up and handed it to him, speechless with joy.

"The Mothers of Invention. *We're Only In It For the Money.* Unbelievable choice, Tim! Come to think of it, no one has ever chosen it before. And it's one of my real favorites." Looking at Thomas, Dr. Amato continued fondling the record, "This is so cool. Particularly side one. "What's the Ugliest Part of Your Body?" is so right on. "And Who Needs the Peace Corps?" kills me. Thomas, we are in for a real treat. Thank you, Tim. Thank you. You've made my day. Did you know that many of Frank's bandmates have played in philharmonic orchestras?"

He had to be drugged out of his mind. He was a completely different person. Or I was having an amazing dream. Maybe I had finally slipped into the Twilight Zone.

Looney continued, "So now, Thomas, if you would be so kind as to put on side one, I'll tell Tim about today's procedure."

And so it went. The shots that numbed my mouth didn't hurt a bit. It seemed like Looney kept a perfect beat to the music while breaking my wisdom teeth apart. And two other things: he no longer had bad breath, and his humming had improved dramatically. He was actually in tune and frequently harmonizing! The two of them worked like a smooth, well-tuned team, smiling the entire time.

When it was all over, Dr. Amato (I will never call him Looney again) thanked me one more time for my musical choice and then wrote me a prescription for codeine. "Since you're obviously an aficionado of music, I strongly recommend that you check out Buffy St. Marie's version of "Codeine." It's a real eye opener about the plight of our Indian friends. Treat yourself."

After handshakes all around, I walked out into the reception area beaming and gave my dad a great big hug. I hadn't hugged him like that since I was a kid, desperately trying anything to avoid going to the first day of nursery school. I turned to salute Grace, and she saluted right back and threw in a thumb's up. She looked like she might jump up on her desk, she was so thrilled. Dad had no idea what to make of the apparent love fest.

I will never fear a dental office again. At least not Dr. Amato's. What album should I choose the next time I go to see him?

Coleville of the Dale

Sir John Coleville is one of many minor characters in Shakespeare's *Henry IV, Part II*. But don't tell him that.

Now, you should probably know that I had never acted before. My English professor told all of us with a B or less at midterm in his Shakespeare class that we should strongly consider auditioning for the upcoming college play, *Henry IV, Part II*. I had a low B and thought why not? What's there to lose? So I tried out and got the part of Sir John Coleville. One scene. "Scene Three, Act IV." Pretty easy way to lock up a B if you ask me.

Here's my assessment of Sir John. This guy was a very powerful, fearless "soldier." He was ready to die for the rebel cause. Anything to defeat the royalists! Prince Hal's buddy and Coleville's soon-to-be-opponent, Falstaff, had an unfounded reputation for being fearless as well. In reality, he was an opportunistic drunk who had no interest in fighting, just boasting. Truth be told, he was terrified of battle. And yet, Sir John and the other rebels had heard just the opposite – that Falstaff was a monstrous fighting machine. Someone you didn't mess with – not even Coleville!

So, if I was going to be true to Sir John, I would be ready and able to maul anyone I confronted in the dale – just another straightforward ass kicking - until I found out it was Falstaff.

The play was very well received by the college and local community. A good run, as our director called it. The last night was no exception. The place was packed with students, faculty, and townies.

Our scene began simply enough, just like the other nights. I entered from stage right, swinging my sword around, looking for my next victim. This was war! Falstaff came on five or so seconds later from stage left, looking terrified of the unknown dangers lurking in the spooky Forest of Gaultree, his back to me.

That was my cue to charge up a riser and challenge him to the duel of all duels. It wasn't that big a riser. Four steps up to a landing. No more than three and a half feet off the ground. Our director thought it would be very imposing ("the height will convey a sense of size and power") and that the audience would instantly know the immense strength of Coleville – how "imposing a figure he truly was." I loved it.

At this point, you probably need to know that I was stoned. Really stoned. This particular species of evil weed was called "one hit wonder" and it was all over campus that spring. And it really was one-hit-and-you're-stoned weed. I think I had two or three hits. I have no idea what was in it. Let's just say I was so stoned I really thought I was Sir John Coleville of the Dale.

I started up the riser. One step. Two steps. It seemed like I was climbing Mt. Everest, not a riser (that I had helped build) in a play. Three steps. Four steps. I was exhausted, but I had reached the top!

I very slowly and very carefully turned around on the platform, suddenly terribly afraid of the height. It was if I had never been this high in my life. I must have stood there for 10 seconds (it felt like hours). Looking down at the stage floor and then out at the audience (which appeared more like a deep, dark forest in my current state).

It was then that I got an overwhelming desire to jump. Not to bound down the steps as I was supposed to do.

So I jumped. Just as Falstaff turned around to see me for the first time, never in the world expecting me to jump.

It wasn't your basic jump. I let loose with a blood curdling cry, and then leapt off, throwing my sword into the abyss, screaming all the way down (all three and a half feet). It felt like I was hurtling off a cliff, thrusting forward with all my might, hoping to clear the cliff face on the way down. Hoping to land in water hundreds of feet below.

Several of my friends were in the audience. Many of them were tripping or, at the very least, stoned like me. Most of them fled for the exit the moment I screamed and jumped. Screaming as well. Several didn't return. Others peeked back in to see if I had been killed by the fall. A few creeped back in hesitantly.

Oh yeah, I forgot to tell you that the guy playing Falstaff, Tony Alexander, was tripping on acid. Pretty much on a dare. It was the last night of the show, and he figured, "What could possibly go wrong? I know my lines. Everyone else does, too. Piece of cake." So he dropped just before the end of "Act II" and was flying by the time he ran into the airborne Sir John Coleville of the Dale.

Falstaff was supposed to see Coleville and immediately begin running away, then stop, from a safe distance, and ask me who I was. Then I was supposed to answer him, realize that he was Falstaff and then come down from the platform to surrender.

But that's not the way it went down. When I screamed and jumped, Falstaff took off. I mean he really took off. He ran right off the stage, screaming at the top of his lungs. Later he told me he was so freaked out, he wasn't planning to ever go back on stage. He said all he could do was pray that, some day, he would come down from his acid trip and begin his long road to recovery, promising never to use drugs again.

I almost yelled, "Tony, get your ass back in here. Don't do this to me!" But then I realized he had every right to flee. I would have done the same thing if I'd been down there on the ground watching this maniacal guy with a sword jump off a cliff. Hell, in his state, I would have probably died of a heart attack right there on the spot.

So, I was left there on the stage all by myself. I had landed, miraculously in one piece, and was thrilled to be alive after such an incredible jump. But now, suddenly, I was also acutely aware of what was going on around me. Who knows how long I was out there. My choices of what to do next were limited by my state of mind: (1) flee stage left and pretend to chase after Falstaff, (2) flee stage right, displaying fear equal to or greater than the fear Falstaff had shown, (3) bound around on stage acting victorious, waving to the onlookers and fans, or (4) pretend the audience couldn't see me and just nonchalantly walk off. I was leaning toward the latter.

I learned later that, at this moment, the Stage Manager, having just learned of Falstaff's drug-induced condition, was desperately trying to convince him that (1) it was safe to go back on stage, (2) Sir John Coleville was OK (he hadn't died from the fall), (3) this was just a play, and (4) it was Sir John Coleville out there, not the Devil. He was having absolutely no luck.

Fortunately, Tony and I were both saved by the audience. Turns out there were several students who were (a) stoned and (b) had not already fled, sitting there in stunned silence. And then, out of nowhere, one of them stood up and started yelling and clapping wildly. He was immediately joined by 20 to 30 others, and soon by the rest of the audience. This was real theatre! This was Shakespeare performed the way Shakespeare was meant to be performed. Kick ass Shakespeare! One friend ranked our performance right up there with *Fantasia* as the best thing he'd ever seen on drugs. Rich praise indeed.

It was my first standing ovation. I was in total shock. Should I stop and take a bow? Should I stay in character, pick up my sword (where was my sword?), and salute the throngs of fellow rebels? Or should I step out of character and throw it open to an impromptu question-answer period with the audience, to field questions like:

> Did you specifically audition for the Coleville role?
>
> Was it your artistic choice to jump? If so, what was it about Coleville's character that lead you to this decision?
>
> In your opinion, is Coleville a tragic character?
>
> Do you have plans to audition for any upcoming shows?

Of course, now I started obsessing about my sword. I frantically scanned the whole stage and finally saw it (what seemed like a minute was probably five seconds) out front on the left edge of the stage. Later a friend told me that I'd thrown it ("way the fuck up in the air, man") and that it spun around several times before landing with a huge thud about five feet from where Falstaff normally would have been standing (if he hadn't freaked and run off stage when I screamed and jumped). I'm sure Tony/Falstaff would have dropped dead from sheer fright if he been there when the sword landed.

But the applause saved the day. Tony, true to his understanding of Falstaff's ego, could not resist the attention, and came back out on stage. The entire audience went nuts. Huge applause. Shouts. Bravos. Whistling. A few even yelled, "Actor, Actor!"

Tony and I looked at each other. He was no longer Falstaff. He was Tony, my friend, dressed like some weird, overweight buffoon. I started to laugh and had to turn away momentarily to regroup. We somehow delivered our lines flawlessly. I told him I was Sir John Coleville of the Dale, guessed he was Falstaff, and "in that thought yield me." Lancaster, in tears from laughing so hard, appeared out of nowhere, and Falstaff bragged to him about how he had, in his "most pure and immaculate valor, taken Sir John Coleville of the Dale, a most furious knight and valorous enemy." I had a couple more lines I don't remember delivering. I do remember looking out at the audience. Many of them were still standing. And off I was led to be executed.

Ah, the theatre. Long live the King! The son-of-a-bitch gave me a C.

Depresso's List

The first list was posted on the Chapel door, the fourth Monday morning of the fall semester, with a brief note. "Some call this dark or depressing music. I choose to believe this music defines these times and the way our generation views them."

That first list had songs on the subject of "love gone bad" that many of us would have come up with on our own. "Yesterday" and "Ticket To Ride," Roy Orbison's "Crying," Peter and Gordon's Go "To Pieces" (one of my real favorites), "Go Now" by the Moody Blues, "Go Away" by Steve Lawrence (the first 45 I ever bought), "Breaking Up Is Hard To Do" (Neil Sedaka), and Joni Mitchell's "Both Sides Now."

However, at the bottom of the list was a song I'd never heard of. Neither had any of my friends. With that one song he had us. And I'll bet he knew it. The local record store was overwhelmed by requests for "Send The Marines" by Tom Lehrer.

He (I was sticking with "he"…after all, it was an all men's college) posted a new list every Monday morning for eight straight weeks, choosing a new location each week. And each list had at least one song or album that none of us knew. All you had to do was walk around campus early in the morning. Wherever a large crowd of people had gathered was where his latest list would be found.

There was a Joni Mitchell week (he used her birth name, Roberta Joan Anderson) complete with great covers of her songs done by Tom Rush ("Urge for Going") and Dave Van Ronk ("Both Sides Now"). And a drug week (including Buffy Sainte-Marie's "Codeine," Jefferson Airplane's "White Rabbit," "Mother's Little Helper" by the Stones, the Velvet Underground's "Heroin," and Dave Van Ronk's "Cocaine"). I was very pleased to see he had omitted "Puff the Magic Dragon" and "Along Comes Mary."

The 50s week was a classic ("Leader of the Pack," "Tell Laura I Love Her," "Dead Man's Curve," "Teen Angel," and "Last Kiss") with another obscure wonder, "Laurie (Strange Things Happen)," by Dickey Lee. He also posted a few depresso politico lists with such doozies as Buffalo Springfield's "For What It's Worth," Dylan's "The Times They Are A Changin'," Laura Nyro's "Save the Country," Pete Seeger's "Where Have All the Flowers Gone," "Eve of Destruction" by Barry McGuire, Buffy's "Universal Soldier," Simon and Garfunkel's "Sounds of Silence," Dion's "Abraham, Martin and John," and, again catching us off guard, recommended Tom Lehrer's entire album, *That Was the Year That Was*, one week, *All the News That's Fit to Sing* by Phil Ochs another week, and Leonard Cohen's *Songs*

From a Room another. All three of those became immediate hits on campus, blasting out dorm and fraternity windows campus-wide at all times of the day and late into the night.

He also turned us on to albums that had just come out that fall. In the case of *Hot Rats* (Mothers of Invention) and *New York Tendaberry* (Laura Nyro), he even beat announcements by *Rolling Stone, Beat Monthly* and *Billboard*. He was like a prophet.

He single-handedly brought fame to Aum (*Blues Vibes*) and Pentangle (*Basket of Light*) in central Indiana. And Captain Beefheart's *Trout Mask Replica* and Boz Scaggs (title by the same name) quickly reached cult status on campus.

Everyone was going nuts trying to find out who he was. A fraternity even posted guards at all the campus buildings one Sunday night to catch him. It didn't work.

The amazing thing is that no one took any of his lists down. We had that much respect for what he was doing – for us. People, after about the third week, started putting up lists of their own next to his...always identifying themselves. On one occasion that I know of, he agreed with someone's choice the following week and graciously recognized it. Heck of a guy.

Someone called him the Ambrose Bierce of rock and roll and folk. Worked for me. The *Indianapolis Star* got wind of the story and did a bizarre piece, writing it off as a bunch of frustrated male students looking desperately for anything to do with their idle time. The guy knew nothing about our school.

My money was on Craig Dobson, a senior psych major. A loner who looked like Ichabod Crane's brother. He wore a 50s derby and sometimes walked with a cane, though he didn't need it. He wore sunglasses all the time. Indoors and out, no matter what the weather. He smoked Newports. No one smoked Newports. Kools, "Reds," even Tareytons, but not Newports. You get the idea. But here's the kicker. He didn't seem to do any of these things intentionally. That was just Craig. Case closed in my humble opinion. Except he didn't select Simon and Garfunkel's "I Am A Rock," a song that he could have written about himself.

In mid November came another really cool thing. Professor Grimes in the Music Department invited the "depresso phantom" to guest lecture. Acutely aware of the interest this person had piqued in faculty and students alike, Grimes announced the class would be held in the campus theatre on the first Tuesday night in December. Seating 750 plus.

It was packed. Standing room only. No one was late. It's the only class or lecture I had ever attended like that.

Grimes had done it right. When we showed up, he had someone manning a turntable, piping in songs off the phantom's lists.

Promptly at 7:30, Grimes walked out onto the stage and up to the podium. To much applause, I might add. He had become an instant celebrity in his own right after deciding to do this.

"Hello everyone. And welcome to what I hope is a very special evening." The *Indianapolis Star* had a guy there snapping photos of Grimes and the crowd. I guess they couldn't resist either.

"First, I want you to know that I have not had contact with our new celebrity. I'm like you. I just showed up tonight hoping he will identify himself and perhaps talk to us for a few moments. And, in the best of all worlds, maybe answer some questions. To spice up the deal, I have a speaker's fee I would like to offer him as a way of showing our appreciation for what he has done."

He got another solid round of applause. Even a few whistles.

"Without further adieu, I hope I may have the distinct honor of introducing our featured speaker. He is well known to all of you here tonight. I don't think I exaggerate when I say he has taken this academic community by storm. Monday has taken on an entirely new meaning for all of us, thanks to him. He has us listening to a lot of unfamiliar but significant music, and he even has many of us composing our own lists. In short, he has done something very important for all of us and for this school – he has brought us all together. So, on behalf of our college, please accept our most sincere thanks."

And with that Dr. Grimes walked off the stage and sat down in the front row next to Dr. Warrick, the Dean of Students. That's when I noticed the composition of the audience. Lots and lots of faculty as well as students. And several people that must have been townies.

We all sat there for perhaps two minutes. The first minute you could hear a pin drop. The second minute was full of lots of whispering. Some jerk to my right stood up and was greeted with several gasps. He waved at everyone and sat back down again to boos, embarrassed and also a bit flattered.

Craig Dobson was seated near the front. I kept my eye on him, waiting for him to stand and walk up onto the stage. He never moved.

A couple of people got up and walked out. One guy stood up and said what a lot of others must have been thinking, "He isn't going to show. This is a waste of time." He left as well.

They were all wrong. Our hero had timed it perfectly. By the time he stood up, most people had concluded it wasn't going to happen. He was seated on the aisle in the fifth row, stage left. There were gasps. "Holy shit, it's McEvoy!" Then wild cheers. We had our man. And we kept clapping and cheering.

He calmly walked up the aisle carrying a small note-pad and pen. When he got to the podium, he leaned slightly into the microphone. "Hello, my name is John McEvoy. I'm a junior and, as you can obviously tell, I love music. Especially what many of you now refer to as "depresso" music. To me of course, it's not depresso music. To me, it's the music of the gods of reality. It's our generation's musical answer to all the insanity and madness in the world and here at home. It's an escape to some. It's a constant reminder to others. No more. No less."

The place went nuts. It was like being at the Creedence concert at Butler the night they went on before the Turtles and absolutely destroyed us all. So much so, the Turtles were booed when they came out on the stage. And they were the hottest group in America at the time!

When the crowd collected itself, McEvoy, without saying another word, took a harmonica out of his pocket and proceeded to play a medley of several of the songs he'd put on lists throughout the fall. Just enough of each song that we smiled and nodded acknowledgement. It looked like he was watching us, and, when we got the song, he'd move on to the next one. No one applauded until he was finished, and then the place went nuts again.

"I'm not sure why I'm a celebrity, but I accept that I am. I would like to thank Dr. Grimes for inviting me to speak this evening. That was a very gracious gesture on his part, very atypical of the kinds of things that happen on a daily basis on this campus. I think he deserves a big round of applause." Grimes got just that. After we stopped clapping, McEvoy continued, "And, by the way, I will take him up on his offer of the speaker fee. I can use the money as much as the next guy. I've got records to buy!" More applause and laughter.

For the next 15 minutes, he talked about the music and the artists themselves, and he spoke candidly about his political beliefs, what this school and his friends meant to him, and what had caused him to start making the lists in the first place.

He was the best lecturer I had ever heard. He was incredibly relaxed, he was incredibly knowledgeable, and his delivery was smooth and entertaining. He used the whole stage, too, intentionally walking around to make personal contact with as many people as possible. I had no idea if he'd ever spoken publicly before in his life. How he could do what he did just blew my mind.

"I have one last thought to leave you with. Yesterday was my last posting. As with anything, it's time to move on. I challenge each and every one of you here tonight to find something you love to do and do it. Just like I did. Immediately. Don't wait to be given permission. Don't listen to others who say you aren't ready or don't know enough. Just start. You're running out of time. Thank you."

And with that, he walked off the stage, to a standing ovation and deafening applause. Halfway up the aisle, he stopped, raised his arms to quiet the crowd, and said, "And remember, 'Oh Mama, can this really be the end.'" And he paused for us all to join in, "To be stuck inside of Mobile with the Memphis blues again." The place erupted again, maybe the loudest yet. And he continued singing as he walked out. "Well Shakespeare he's in the alley with his pointed shoes and his bells. Speaking to some French girl who says she knows me well…"

His work was done. Assignment in hand, ours had just begun.

Respecting Privacy

There are a few ordinary jocks that go to school here, a few ordinary brains, and a few ordinary ho-hum types. But the majority of the student body is very, very unordinary.

Not sure why that is or why they ended up here. Maybe it's a haven for all of us. It's not important. What's important is that this place is the perfect backdrop for some truly exceptional insanity.

And though there's no way of knowing for sure (I'm only a sophomore after all) Steven Treski, my roommate, sure appears to be the poster child of this unordinariness.

Steven was already a walking encyclopedia of historical events and data by the time he got to college. I asked him once why he didn't major in history. In between mumblings, he said he knew more about history than any of the profs, and it would be "an utter waste of time for me and an embarrassment to them." I believed him. Point of fact, Steven was the only one who ever tested out of taking freshman World Civilization. The only one. Ever.

Nothing else but history interested him though and so,

by the end of sophomore year, he still hadn't declared a major. That was odd in itself. Of course it was equally insane that all of the rest of us had declared majors when we knew so little about ourselves and our real passions. Most of us had chosen majors based on what our parents did for a living (or what they thought we should do) or what majors our friends had already chosen.

Not Steven. He was determined to test the limits of the system. "I'm only here because my parents want me to get a college degree. And if that's the case, my major doesn't really matter, does it?" It made sense. I was tempted to undeclare.

One night at a party, one of the few ordinary students said to Steven, "But if you don't declare a major, how do you know what you'll be and what you'll do when you leave here?" Steven got up, shook his head, gave me a look of disgust, and walked out without saying a word. Something in him had snapped.

Soon after that he started dressing differently. His baggy pants and blue jean jacket gave way to an old Army jacket and fatigues from the Salvation Army store. He started eating most of his meals out of cans. And he started obsessing about the Vietnam War. One of his professors even suggested he seek counseling.

Art, our other roommate, stopped me at Steven's bedroom door one evening. "You've got to see this." And he started to open the door.

"We can't go in there," I objected. "That's an invasion of Steven's privacy."

"I'll show you invasion." And he opened it.

The south and east walls of Steven's room were painted Army green. On the south wall, in bold black lettering, was a Vietnam timeline including a list of recent events. On the east wall was a list of other important dates that highlighted such things as France's involvement in Vietnam.

1944-1945	Japanese invade; French Vichy Government serves as Japanese puppet
1945-1946	British troops in country
1946-1954	First Indochina War (French)
1954	Geneva Convention creates two Vietnams
1955	Ngo Dinh Dien leader of new Republic of Vietnam
1959	Second Indochina War (French)
May, 1961	Kennedy sends Green Berets to train South Vietnamese soldiers
October, 1961	Kennedy sends additional military "advisers" to Vietnam
November 1963	President Diem is assassinated
March, 1965	LBJ sends first U.S. combat troops to Vietnam
January, 1968	Tet Offensive
August 17-26, 1969	Battle of Que Son Valley
September 2, 1969	Death of Ho Chi Minh
September 21, 1969	B52's drop more than 1000 tons of bombs on North Vietnam near DMZ
November 3, 1969	Nixon speech to his "Silent Majority" for support
November 16, 1969	First mention of My Lai

On the north wall Steven had drawn a very detailed

map of Vietnam. To the right of his door he had sketched a plane spraying something he'd labeled agent orange. And to the left of the door was a drawing of a destroyed hut with bodies scattered all around.

I was shocked. "What the hell is going on?'

"I think we need to talk to him. Our landlord will evict us if he sees this."

"No shit."

When we confronted him later that night, Steven said it was no big deal. And if the landlord saw it, Steven said he would tell him that he planned to repaint all the walls in his bedroom at the end of the semester. Art and I both ended up writing it off as odd behavior from a well-established odd person.

I was alone in our house two weeks later when a cop knocked on the door. Suddenly paranoid that I was about to be busted for possession, I asked him in my shakiest voice what I could do for him.

"I'm Sergeant Warren. Can I come in?'

I paused to consider my rights. He knew what I was thinking. My quivering voice told him everything he needed to know. My mind raced ahead – who would I make my one phone call to from jail?

"You're Daniel, aren't you? Don't worry. This isn't a bust. I need to talk to you about one of your roommates, Joseph Steven Tresnick."

How the hell did he know who I was? Not good. And I didn't even know Steven was actually Joseph Steven.

"Sure," I stammered and opened the door for him to enter.

He did a quick scan of the living room, like all the cops in the movies do, and then said, "When's the last time you saw him?"

My head was spinning. Good question. Not today. Not yesterday either, come to think of it.

"Two days ago, I believe."

He sat down in the big chair that our friend, Jeff, sat in to roll his famous joints. There were probably hundreds of seeds on and under the chair cushion.

"We found him north of town by the railroad tracks."

"Found him? Is he...?"

"No, he's not dead."

"Notice anything odd about him recently?"

"Odd? It would be more remarkable if I noticed anything normal."

Looking into the hallway, he continued his cross-examination. "Does Joseph have his own room?"

I nodded.

"Mind if I have a look inside?" He started walking down the hallway.

"Well, it's off limits to us. He doesn't want us invading his privacy."

"We're past that now. Have you been in it lately?"

"Maybe a couple of weeks ago." And I told him about the walls.

I opened Steven's door, and he walked inside. The map was even more beautiful and complete, and a couple of other items had been added to the timeline.

More disturbing, however, was a huge pile of dirt on the floor. A shovel, garden trowel, a chisel, a hammer and two large Maxwell Coffee cans were carefully arranged on the edge of a large piece of cloth next to the dirt pile.

The cop walked over, lifted the cloth up and motioned for me to join him. The cloth had been covering a hole in the floor. A big hole. Big enough for Steven to crawl into. The flooring had been removed. So had the sub flooring and whatever was underneath that.

"This is how he got out. How he escaped."

"What do you mean, escaped?"

"He thinks he is an escaped POW." And, deciding I had no idea what that stood for, he added, "Prisoner of war."

"I know that."

"We got a call. Someone saw smoke coming from north of town along the railroad tracks. When we got there, your roommate was sitting by a fire. He had a sleeping bag, some books, and it looked like he'd cooked a couple of meals."

I didn't know what to say.

"He was really glad to see us. He acted like we'd gotten to him just before the Cong did."

"Where's he right now?"

"He's been admitted into the psychiatric ward at the hospital for his own safety. No visitors. They're trying to get him stabilized."

"Is he OK?"

"No. Right now, he thinks he's being debriefed, so that's the way the doctors are treating him."

Steven's parents came to get his stuff the next day even though there wasn't much left. He'd gotten rid of all his other clothes. There were a few books (he had a couple hundred before), a toothbrush and toothpaste, and what was left of a quart of black paint. He'd obviously unloaded just about everything else he owned.

His parents weren't very communicative. Said it was a family matter. His father said he would send us some money for Steven's portion of the rent and utilities through the end of the term.

I got a letter from Steven two weeks later. No return address and no date. It sounded like it had been written before the police found him.

> *Hey,*
>
> *It's nuts over here and hotter than the devil's domicile. Soaking wet from the humidity. Gotta stay high just to survive. Last night was my turn for night duty, and it scared the shit out of me like it always does. I kept sensing one of them was real close, about to take me down.*
>
> *This is insanity. I'll let you in on a little secret. If I ever get out of here alive, I know what I'm going to major in – Far Eastern history.*
>
> *Not wishing you were here.*
>
> *Steven*

He's going to be a history major after all.

E.V.A.N.S.

A tall black guy, maybe 6'4", was shooting baskets in the alley behind our apartment. I'd been watching him out our kitchen window for five minutes or so. Smooth shot. Picture perfect release. Great dribbler. Dipping in and out, faking out his imaginary opponent and throwing up shot after shot that went in.

I decided to go outside and watch. He hit a fade away shot from the left corner and saw me as he retrieved the ball underneath the basket, just before it would have rolled down the hill into the alley. He dribbled between his legs, did an around-the-world with the ball, set up his next shot and spoke to me without looking my way.

"Shoot for it?"

"For what?"

"A beer. Six pack. Pint. Whatever you want."

"I don't really drink much," I admitted.

He laughed. "Not a problem, we can play for money." He paused for a moment. "I call it EVANS."

"What?"

"This," pointing at the basketball and the hoop. "EVANS.

After Bill Evans."

"I don't know Bill Evans. Should I?"

"Yeah, you should."

"Are you going to give me a hint?"

"That and more. Much more. And take your money while I'm at it."

He threw me a hard pass. I caught it, though I'm sure he didn't think I would.

"I don't know. I'm pretty busy today."

"How old are you? 19-20?"

"19." I had unconsciously started dribbling the ball and looking up at the rim.

He kept on pushing. "What the fuck do you have to do today that's so god damn important?"

"Classes, homework, test tomorrow. That kind of thing."

"This'll take ten minutes tops. And that's if you can shoot. If you can't, it's over in three."

"I can shoot."

"Never reveal that kind of information to a gamer. Take the first shot."

"Do I get a warm-up or two?"

"If you can shoot as well as you think you can, you don't need any warm-ups." And challenging me, he added, "Haven't you got the touch?"

I took a 15-footer from the left side. It banked off the backboard and went in. He retrieved the ball.

"Intentional?"

"My dad taught me how to bank."

"Once again revealing too much information. Looks

like you shoot out here a lot.

"Some."

"Better. Showing your non-committal side. I like that. Playing it cool. Looks like I may be dealing with a little home court advantage here."

I didn't bite. During this exchange, he had moved over to the same spot where I'd taken my shot and now, calmly, took the shot and missed badly. He didn't seem surprised or even the least bit pissed. I decided it was part of the hustle. Create a sense of false security and then tear me apart.

"That's an E for me. OK. Evans. Bill Evans. Greatest jazz pianist of all time. So, I changed HORSE to EVANS in his honor. Oh, by the way, the other four letters stand for other jazz legends. See, I'm being instructive at the same time I kick your butt."

"But you just missed," I answered.

I took a shot from the same spot. It had worked once, so why not try it again? I missed, almost as badly as he had. He took the rebound, dribbled back to the same spot, and sank the shot.

"All tied up. Two E's. That's more like it."

Surprised by this announcement, I responded, "I don't get a letter for that."

"Chicago street rules. If one guy misses from a spot, and the other guy hits from there, it's a letter. No matter when."

"Sounds like bullshit to me."

He laughed. "Oh, so we've got an attitude. Excellent."

My next shot from the right corner was off, too.

He grabbed the rebound and, instead of going back to that spot, went underneath the basket, turned and took four large steps straight out from it with his back to the rim. There he stopped and threw up an over-the-back shot that swished through the net. Mine went in, too.

He was surprised again. "Nice touch. That shot usually gets me a lot of letters. If nothing else, it usually eliminates a lot of the home court advantage."

"Aren't you revealing too much information now?"

"Touché. Quick learner."

Then I asked him, "So what's your story?"

"Not much to tell," he said, spinning the ball on the tip of his right index finger.

I continued. "How did you end up here?"

When he didn't answer, I dribbled up to the imaginary free throw line and took a jump shot that went in. The ball came back to me, and I did a behind-the-back pass to him. He dribbled over to the same spot, took the jumper and swished it. He flipped the ball to me with the same behind-the-back pass.

Before I could take my next shot, he just started talking.

"Evans played with all the greats and had several bands of his own. Heroin addict, too. Played with Miles Davis on perhaps the best jazz album of all time."

I remained silent, just dribbling around and looking at the basket.

"*Kind of Blue*. 1959. Unbelievable band. Evans, Cannonball, Coltrane, Chambers, Cobb, Kelly. No one has ever been able to touch that sound since, in my humble opinion."

I took another free throw shot and made it.

"Pretty good free throw shooter. Did you play in high school?"

"Yes."

"Just my luck."

He missed his shot. "Damn. V. EV. I must be losing my touch."

"Trying to play the pity card?"

"No, but thanks for the idea."

"Who does V stand for?"

"Today I'd say Sarah Vaughan. Look her up."

"How did you end up here?'

"Let's just say this is one of the stops on my nationwide campus tour."

I was beginning to wonder why I was wasting valuable study time. I sat down on the ball. "Do you play jazz?"

"Very good guess. Yes."

We exchanged shots for a couple of minutes. Everything went in. I finally missed a left-handed flip standing underneath the basket, and he made it.

Now he was acting like he was back in control. "I don't usually play lefties. EV. Excellent. This could take a while. Tell me something interesting about yourself."

"My dad just died."

"Damn, man. Sorry to hear it. When?'

"Just before school started."

He missed his next shot. It looked to me like he wasn't really trying. Maybe he was giving me one.

Shifting gears, I said, "Want a beer?"

"I thought you didn't drink."

"Sometimes I do. We've got a couple in the fridge. Interested?"

Without hesitation he added, "I'm pretty hungry, too."

"PB & J and some fritos are about the best I can do."

"Done."

And inside we went. I fixed two sandwiches, put the bag of fritos on the kitchen table and got two beers out of the fridge while he walked around the apartment.

When he came back into the kitchen, I motioned him to the table.

"So, why are you here?"

"I told you."

"Not good enough."

"My younger brother went here."

"Where's he now?"

Taking a second big slug of beer, he said, "Hell if I know."

I pushed it. "Not good enough."

He tried to change the subject. "What's your major?"

"Biology. So about your brother."

"He's dead."

"Shit." Something clicked in my mind. "Did he die here?"

He nearly fell out of his chair. "Jesus Christ! You're freaking me out, kid. Yeah. He got hit by a car about two blocks from here."

"He was a musician, too, wasn't he?

"Damn, kid. You're spooky. Tenor sax."

I shut up. He started pacing around the kitchen.

"He's buried here. I'll just answer your other questions before you ask them. He died ten years ago today. I'm here to pay my respects. Our old man just sort of lost it after my brother died. Started hitting the booze real hard, and he dropped dead about four years ago. Our mom isn't in much better shape. Walking dead kind of thing, if you know what I mean."

"What do you play?"

"Trumpet."

"Who have you played with?"

He was still pacing. "Chicago scene. You wouldn't know the names." And then, he came right up to me and said, "I don't think I want to finish our little game."

"No problem." I was happy to hear it.

He finished his beer and held up the can. I went to get him the last one from the fridge. He belched and asked me, "You play on the college team?"

"Chose not to. Not a very popular decision I might add. Lost the athletic part of my scholarship."

He sat down again. "Didn't like the coach?"

"Didn't like his offense. He had the same guy shooting all the time, and it was way too predictable. And he was wasting a lot of talent."

"I hate that."

"We had the makings of a fairly good team, too. Two other starters quit the same time I did."

"I could tell you were a player."

"Thought about transferring somewhere else. I may still."

We both stood up at the same time, without speaking,

and started heading back out courtside, beers in hand. We started shooting again, but with no letters at stake. Neither of us could miss. Everything we put up was going in.

After a few minutes, he said, "Next one to get a letter loses?"

"No need."

Now he was pissed. "The hell there isn't!"

"Why?"

Throwing me a hard pass, he responded. "It's not over. We need to finish this, one way or the other."

"Five minutes ago you said you didn't want to finish the game."

"I changed my mind."

I dropped the ball and watched it starting to roll down the incline. "Well, it's over for me."

He couldn't let go. "Chickening out, aren't you. Afraid I'll beat you?"

"Who cares? What's the big deal?"

He picked up the ball and started dribbling it high and hard. "I don't lose. That's what the big deal is."

He took a shot and then pleaded with me, "One more letter, and we'll call it. I promise."

"Fine. What do the other letters stand for? A, N, and S."

"They vary from day to day. Today's answers are Ahmad Jamal for A, Red Norvo for N, and, of course, Satchmo for S."

"Red Norvo?"

"A great vibraphonist who recorded with some of

the legends like Bird, Billy Holiday and Sinatra. You know Jamal?"

"The name rings a bell. Must have been in my older brother's record collection. Piano player, right? I remember his photo on a cover."

"Very impressive."

"Do you make a living playing EVANS or the piano?"

"Neither really. Wait a minute. I didn't tell you I played piano. I told you I played the trumpet."

"Evans did, so I just figured you do, too."

He missed his next shot.

I had another idea. "Call it a tie?"

"You know I was playing with you, right? You know I could kick your butt if I wanted to."

"It's a tie or you lose. And you don't want to lose. You've lost enough already. And, come to think of it, so have I."

He didn't push any farther. "Mind if I stay and shoot some?"

"Fine by me. I don't own the court. Some guy named Evans does."

He laughed loudly. "You're shitting me, right?"

"Yup."

We both smiled and shook hands. I didn't want to spend any more time with him. And he knew it. As I headed toward the back door, he yelled out, "First time I've ever lost at EVANS."

"You didn't lose. We tied."

He wouldn't' let it go. "I lost."

"I would have won if we'd kept playing. Guess that's

why you're saying you lost."

"Bull shit."

"You'll never know." I started back into the house. Without looking back, I said, "Good luck with your music."

"Good luck with your studies, my friend."

I turned to face him. "Marty."

"Joe-Joe," he answered.

I went inside and did some Inorganic homework. When I came out an hour and a half later, he was gone. There was a note propped up at the base of the pole.

"My brother's name was Archie Green. Look him up."

Sammy

His name was Sammy. I have no idea how old he was. Dougy wouldn't say. I always just assumed he was the same age as Dougy. And, boy, were they tight. They went everywhere together. Connected at the hip, you might say.

Dougy is my brother. Sammy was Dougy's imaginary friend. I use that term loosely, because he sure seemed real, even to the rest of us. Mom and I, and to some extent Dad, treated Sammy just like a member of the family. Or as close as we could considering we couldn't see him or interact with him without going through Dougy. Which worked most of the time.

I had some pretty good conversations with Sammy, mainly about sports and high school girls. He knew a hell of a lot about baseball. Come to think of it, he was better than me at batting averages. That amazed me, because I studied them religiously. Sometimes Sammy listened to the Tigers on the radio with Dad and me. Dougy didn't know squat about baseball and wouldn't be caught dead listening to it. Dougy hated sports.

Sammy was the perfect conduit for us to find out

what was going on with Dougy. It was Sammy who told us how Dougy broke his wrist. And it was Sammy who told me about Dougy stealing the candy and balloons at Martin's Drug Store. And the time Dougy threw the brick through Mr. Turner's living room window.

The two of them were inseparable until Dougy turned 12. I think something happened at his birthday party because, overnight it seemed, Sammy was gone. Maybe the two of them had a fight. More likely, Dougy slipped in front of his friends at the party and was exposed. Maybe he thanked Sammy for his birthday present or something, and his buddies made fun of him. See, when he talked to Sammy, Dougy went trance-like and was all eyes and ears. That wouldn't have gone over really well with a bunch of 12-year-old boys who probably didn't even want to be at this weird kid's house in the first place. Dougy stopped hanging out with them – further proof that something had happened.

Whatever the case, the break-up was really tough on Dougy and, I assume, on Sammy. Of course, Dougy wouldn't talk about it. For us it was like a death in the family. For about a month, Dougy was in a real funk. But then Doug (we had to stop calling him Dougy about the same time) recovered and moved on.

Now, nearly seven years later, Sammy's back. Maybe he never left, but I think I would have known that. Anyways, I got this really odd call tonight at school from Dougy. "Hey, Dave. It's Dougy (no longer Doug). Sammy says hi."

I instantly went on red alert.

"Really?"

"Yeah. Really. Want to ask him anything?"

"Ah, sure. Yeah. OK." I was way out of practice. "Where have you been, Sammy?"

There was the same old pause I remember so well from when we were kids.

"He says, 'No place special. Here and there. You know, just groovin' the scene, man.'"

"I had no idea Sammy was so hip."

"He's hip alright. Ask him something else."

This was Dougy's way of getting me to ask Sammy what was going on. He did that a lot when we were kids.

"How long have you been back?"

"He got in last night. I called him." Dougy wasn't helping much.

"I wanna talk to Sammy, Dougy."

"Shit, Dave. He didn't really call me. He sort of tracked me down, I'd say."

It had happened. I was now talking to Sammy. His voice was much deeper than it used to be, but still slower paced than Dougy's. It was definitely Sammy.

"So what did Dougy tell you?"

"That he missed me. And that he was in trouble and needed my help."

"What kind of trouble, Sammy?"

"Well, for starters, he said he'd slashed the tires on some professor's truck."

"Is he in trouble for that?"

"He told me they'll never catch him."

"What are you doing right now, Sammy?"

Sammy laughed. "I'm talking to you, Dave!"

"You said 'for starters.' What's that mean?"

"He doesn't want you to know about the other things, Dave. Sorry."

"What other things, Sammy?"

"No idea, but they must be bad if he won't even tell me."

"Are you in his dorm room?"

"No."

"Is there anyone else with you besides Dougy."

"Your mom's here and so is this other nice lady. She's dressed kinda like a nurse."

Sammy was still a kid. "Can I speak to Mom?"

There was an uncomfortable silence.

"Hey, Sammy?"

"Yeah, Dave."

"Good talking to you. I'm glad you're back."

"Thanks, Dave. Good talking to you, too. Long time, huh."

One of them handed the phone to Mom.

"Hi, Davey."

"Hi, Mom."

"Sorry about that. Sammy insisted on calling you. The school called me yesterday. Dougy's apparently had another episode. So we've brought him home and admitted him here at Singleton."

"I'll come home tonight."

"No need, Honey. He's right where he needs to be right now. Safe as can be. There isn't really anything you could do anyway. Really. Believe me."

"Are you OK?"

"Thank goodness Sammy's here."

"Yup."

"Sammy wants to say something else to you. Here he is. And, Honey, don't worry."

Sammy took the phone. "Dave, this is the year. We're going to the World Series. Our pitching's back. It's time to win one for Kaline!"

"You're absolutely right, Sammy. Hope to see you soon."

"Catch you later, Dave. Stay cool! Lolich is on the mound tonight against Horlen."

Sing Praises Unto Our King

The grand old church. That's what everyone calls it. Not really that old by world standards. Or by classic American standards for that matter. But compared to the other churches covering every other inch of this town, it is truly grand and old.

I've walked by St. Luke's Church many, many times and never had any desire, or need, to go inside. That was, until my English comp professor said, "Explore spaces and places unfamiliar to you. Discover what they offer. See what they have to say to you." St. Luke's fit the bill perfectly for me.

See, I spent my childhood and teenage Sunday mornings in a church also named St. Luke's. It was a prerequisite for family membership. I was there for them, my parents and their friends. Not for me. As a result, I tuned out most of the doctrine and proselytizing. All of it, in fact, except the music.

Not because it was great music. It wasn't. The adult choir was mediocre at best. Even the lead soprano missed notes on a frequent basis. The choirmaster, however, was an excellent organist and could cover

over much of what the voices lacked. And occasionally he did a long solo that was amazing.

The congregational faithful, lacking my sophisticated ear, were always very appreciative of the music. They were moved by the average harmonies and spotty solos and comforted by the personal messages they heard in the lyrics. And they belted out the choruses when it was their turn to open their hymnals and sing along. Some of their harmonies were even quite good, including my father's. Others were forgettable (my mother's). Many others out and out sucked, but that certainly didn't stop them from letting loose in that hallowed and safe setting.

The boys' choir, however, which usually had six to ten members, had its moments. The voices ranged from boys' soprano to transition tenors and baritones. Most of them were unable to hit the higher registers anymore, but were not yet entirely comfortable at the lower registers either. And, because of that vocal limbo, they were capable of producing some truly eerie sounds.

I was a member of that boys' choir for two years and loved every moment of it. We were damn good, especially the first year I was a member. Four of us were at near perfect boy soprano range, and we could sing the socks off the rest of the choir. Our choirmaster knew it, too, and gave us far more solos than the adults. It really pissed them off. And during the Christmas season, civic groups would request visits from the boys' choir, not the full choir.

I quit when it was no longer cool to be in the choir

(which coincided nicely with when my voice changed in junior high). When it was time to start dreaming of bashing heads on the football field and fantasizing about going out with high school seniors named Martha and Louise.

I stopped going to church entirely when I went off to college. My mother was fine with it. She stopped going, too, and my father was crushed. Satan had won over two more converts. Dad actually told me once that he would pray for our souls. He would have been happy to know I had finally seen the light and returned.

There were no lights on in the church's inner sanctum. Because of the dark, dreary morning, there was very little natural light coming in through the huge stain-glass windows. I started walking forward from the narthex. It was a very large building with a gorgeous Gothic revival sanctuary. It could easily seat 750 worshippers. I could almost see them streaming in on Sunday morning, all decked out in their Sunday finest. I sat down in a pew about 12 rows up and flopped over to look up at the ceiling, waiting to be blessed with a writing topic or two.

And then, out of nowhere, I heard an exquisite sound. I couldn't identify where it was coming from, but I knew what it was instantly. A boy's voice. He was singing. Pitch perfect. He had to be nine or ten.

It was the most beautiful boy's voice I'd ever heard. The boy was somewhere up in the alter area, perhaps in one of the choral pews. I didn't dare sit up to get a better look and risk frightening him or scaring him away.

He sang the first two verses of "Holy, Holy, Holy." Then he sang a verse from several standard hymnal songs. "I'll Fly Away." "Blessed Assurance." "Precious Memories." "Wayfaring Stranger." A medley, if you will, of songs from different Christian denominations. He was testing his pitch, listening to the echo of his voice, and playing with the acoustics in the church. Gauging his breathing capacity. Experimenting. And it was glorious. It was all I could do not to join in. Or at least cheer loudly.

The little cherub mixed his singing in with some gorgeous whistling, too, and the sounds resonated throughout the church as well as every cell in my body. After four minutes or so of this virtuoso performance, he suddenly went silent. One minute. Two minutes. I thought perhaps he'd left, but I hadn't heard any foot-steps. Had he heard me?

Just when I decided the boy had left, he started whis-tling again. Five distinct notes. Five notes I knew. Four words that corresponded with those five notes sat pre-cariously on the edge of my vocal cords, ready to escape joyfully. Then he stopped. Twenty seconds later he repeated the same five notes.

I couldn't hold the words in any longer so I sang out in my best tenor voice (which is pretty decent if I don't mind saying so myself).

"I'm telling you now."

Silence. And then, from the boy came, "I know it's been said before."

I took a deep breath and responded, "Say you love

me, and I will be sure."

He was more than up to the challenge. "I'm in love with you now."

Silence.

And then, as if perfectly arranged, we started singing the next line at the exact same moment. He deserved the lead and took it, so I harmonized on the phrase.

"Do you think I'm fooling when I say I love you?"

We kept going. "I love you. Maybe you'll believe me when I'm finally through."

Then we switched back and forth with the "throughs."

"Through, through, through."

And then we sang together. I threw in a little more harmony for good measure on the final verse.

"I'm telling you now, I know it's been said before. Say you'll love me and I will be sure. I'm in love with you now. I'm telling you now."

Silence. I just stood there taking in the moment. After awhile, I knew it was time to leave. As I started to tip-toe out, the boy clapped. I hope he took a bow. He was good enough to be the lead in the Vienna Boys' Choir.

I walked out into the cool, overcast afternoon and immediately started dancing "The Freddie"…sticking my left leg and arms out, pulling them back in, sticking out my right leg and arms, and so on, humming the Freddie and the Dreamers' classic. No one seemed to notice or, if they did, they completely ignored me.

A month later I was at Kroger's buying my college student staples - fritos, onion dip, cheddar cheese, sliced ham, mayonnaise, bread, cereal, milk and tomato juice. I was third in line behind an Episcopal priest who was fidgeting in his pocket for change, and a young boy, swaying gently from side to side to an inner rhythm. He was looking at the ground, not making eye contact with anyone.

Five soft, pitch-perfect notes came whistling out of the boy's mouth.

Without hesitation, I responded with seven.

His head came up, and we made eye contact.

Nine notes together.

And then his solo. Six notes.

We nodded to each other.

The priest, who I guessed must be his father, was totally oblivious. So was the cashier.

The boy did some spins as he started heading out the door with the priest. Just before they reached the door, he looked back at me over his left shoulder once more and started whistling the song as loudly as he could.

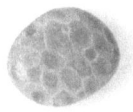

Down Five With Six Minutes to Go

I just went to the basement to transfer some laundry from the washing machine to the dryer. I keep telling my husband, Walt, that we need to replace both machines. Gosh, I'll bet they're 15 years old. Maybe even 20. And now, when I come back upstairs, Walt isn't in his chair in the living room. He's always there this time of day. Looking at the paper. Humming something from *South Pacific* or *Mahagony*. Looking through his *TV Guide* even though he has no intention of watching anything. Sales magazines scattered on his ottoman (he never uses it to put his feet up on). He's still getting complimentary issues even though he's been retired for over ten years and doesn't read them anymore.

Let me tell you, he used to be a big reader. I throw out a bunch every month and put the new ones in the old ones' place. He doesn't seem to notice.

Walt's chair has seen better days. The springs must have given out a long time ago. So there's this permanent indentation, more like a crater actually, where he's sat for who knows how long. When I asked him a few years back if he would like to get it reupholstered, he was particularly short with me. "No! What's wrong with it?" He's never that short with me. I won't offer again.

Sorry. I digress. Now I've come into the kitchen to see if he's sneaking a peek at what's in the refrigerator. Walt's very predictable. He's not a very good wrapper so I can usually tell when he's been into something. And he knows nothing about placement so I can also tell if an item or two has been "rearranged."

Favorites of his? That's easy. A swig of maple syrup is one. Once a month or so I have to buy a new bottle. I don't make pancakes that often to warrant running out so fast. A bite of cheese is another. Most of the time he tries to straighten the remaining piece with a knife so it looks normal. Of course, he leaves the knife on the counter after this surgery, and the cut is usually at an odd angle, not like cutting a normal slice. And there's the peanut butter jar. He keeps the inside edges very clean with his finger scraping. Too clean. You get the idea, I'm sure.

Anyways, I just glanced out the kitchen window facing our driveway and garage and the Bakers' house. Walt is out shooting baskets in our driveway! See, we've got a basketball rim attached to our garage above the door. He put it up for the boys 40 years ago. Maybe longer.

He's still in the pajama bottoms and t-shirt he slept in last night, and I'll bet it's probably 25 degrees outside. Definitely not basketball weather. The ball looks like it's lost its bounce. But he sure looks like he's enjoying himself. I haven't seen him this happy in months. I hope his team wins.

Basketball. Baseball. That driveway is full of memories. If I close my eyes, I can still see the kids out there playing. I'm in here making meatloaf or one of my famous pound cakes, or washing dishes, watching them while I work. For eight months of the year I left the window up for the breeze, but also so I could hear what the kids were talking about. On rare occasions, someone mentioned a girl's name or said something about Walt or me or commented on one of their teachers. Otherwise it was all about sports and sports' heroes. It seems like just yesterday. I miss all the commotion.

The phone's ringing.

"Hello?"

"Hi, Mom."

(It's Charley, our youngest. He never calls this time of day. Something's wrong. I know it. His son, Jake, has missed a lot of school this winter. I hope everything's OK.)

"Mom?"

"Hi, Dearest."

"It's Charley. How's Dad?"

"He's fine, Dear. He's outside shooting baskets."

"He's what?"

"Isn't that the silliest thing you've ever heard?"

"Mom, it's cold out there."

"Below freezing, I'm quite sure. And they say it's supposed to get even colder this evening, too."

"Mom."

"And, if you can believe it, he's still in his jammies!"

"Mom."

"Yes, Dear?"

"Is everything OK?"

"Of course, Dear. Why do you ask?"

"Well, I got this odd phone call from Dad last night. Real late."

"What did he say?"

"Hey, Mom, can you do me a favor?"

"Anything for my baby."

"You're in the kitchen, right?"

"Well yes I am. How did you know that, Charley?"

"It's not important. Can you open the window and tell me if you hear anything Dad is saying?"

"Just a second, Honey. I have to put the phone down."

(The window's stiff in this cold. There we go.)

"Honey, are you still there?"

"Yes, Mom. Is Dad saying something?"

"Well, yes he is! Just a second. He's saying something about down by five with six minutes to go. Could that be right?"

"Can you hear if he's announcing any names?"

(Charley is so smart.)

"Cantrell? And someone named Big Bill?"

"OK."

"Who are they, Sweetie?"

"Michigan basketball players. From a few years back."

"I don't remember those names."

"Mom. You need to get Dad inside. It's too cold for him to be out there right now."

"But he seems to be having so much fun."

"He is, Mom. Maybe he needs a break though. Just tell him that lunch is ready."

"But it's not, Charley!"

"Don't worry. That'll get him in. Can you do that for me?"

"Well, yes. I guess I can."

"And Mom?"

"Yes, Dear."

"Don't use his name."

"Right oh, Charley. Oh, it's a game, isn't it! Just a sec. Honey, lunch is ready. Come on in!"

"That was great, Mom."

"It's working, Charley. He just waved to me. And now he's coming in!"

"That's terrific, Mom."

(Charley really is amazing. He always was, come to think of it. He's a special boy. Here comes Walter now!)

"He's inside, Charley. It's Charley, Walter. Want to say hi?"

"Sure thing."

(I just gave Walter the phone.)

"Hey, Charles. How are things?"

"Great, Dad. Who won?"

"It's not over. We were flat in the first half, but we're shooting much better in the second and playing defense like we really mean business."

"Who are we playing?"

"Those damn twins from Indiana."

"The VanArsdales?"

"Yeah. And Darden just fouled out. But don't worry,

Cazzie's on fire right now."

"That's great, Dad."

"Anything wrong, Charles?"

"Just checking in. Give Mom a big kiss for me, will ya?"

"I sure will, Son."

"Dad, will you put Mom back on for a second?"

"You got it, Charles."

"Hope the Maize and Blue pull it out, Dad."

"Thanks, Son. Hail to the Victors! Here's Mom again."

"Mom?"

"Yes, Dear?"

"I love you, Mom."

"And I love you, too, Charley."

"What's for lunch?"

"I was just thinking about that, Dear. I haven't decided for sure, but I may just whip up a batch of pancakes for your father. We haven't had them in quite a while, and you know how all you boys love your pancakes."

"We sure do. Have a couple for me. With lots of syrup."

"I will. If we have any left. You know Dad!"

"I sure do. Well, gotta run, Mom."

"Bye for now then, Sweetheart."

I forgot to ask him how little Jakey is doing. He didn't mention anything, though. That's a good sign, I guess. He'd tell me if something was wrong, wouldn't he? Should I call him back? Or would he just think I was being silly? I'm just trying to be supportive. I know, I'll say a little prayer for Jakey.

Walt is back in his chair with his *TV Guide* humming "Bloody Mary." Now, what was I doing?

Arthur Woodbridge

Arthur Woodbridge died yesterday at the age of 19. He lived in an apartment with a friend of mine, Jonathon Wilson. I knew Arthur from Chemistry lab, freshman year. He was quiet, smart, and always smiling, even if, at times, it looked like it was a forced smile.

According to Jonathon, Arthur kept pretty much to himself. Not that he was standoffish. I think he was just really shy. Like his roommate, Jonathon. They were a perfect match.

Jonathon said Arthur wrote a lot of letters to his girlfriend back home, but the letters he received were from his mom, not his girlfriend. Other than that, the only thing we knew about him was that he loved music.

Jonathon said Arthur always had an album on the stereo. And he knew more about rock and roll and folk than all of us put together. A walking encyclopedia. Which was puzzling, because he didn't have a big album collection, and he didn't subscribe to any music magazines.

Jonathon found Arthur lying in the middle of the living

room floor. Dead. No blood. Just lying there looking completely relaxed and seemingly content. After calling the police, Jonathon called me, and I went right over to see if there was anything I could do to help. The Dean of Students arrived about the same time I did and said he would take care of contacting Arthur's family. Two policemen spent a couple hours looking around the apartment and then left without saying much. Since we weren't "family," all they allowed was that they would know more after the autopsy.

Jonathon was really shook up. And rightfully so. He didn't want to leave the living room, so the two of us just sat and talked. Another friend of ours, Michael Armory, showed up just after the cops had left and said that Arthur hadn't been in Invertebrate Biology class that morning.

That was very strange. Arthur never missed a class.

Then Jonathon noticed a half-full beer on the table beside the turntable, one that hadn't been there last night. Arthur didn't drink.

Arthur's room was spotless, which wasn't normal either. Jonathon said Arthur was a slob in his own room. Not anywhere else in the apartment. Just in his room. But now, the books in his room were neatly stacked. He'd done his laundry, and his clothes were all carefully folded and put away in the dresser. His bed was made (something he never did), and his shoes were all arranged neatly in pairs on his closet floor.

And then there was the goldfish in a bowl on the kitchen table. Jonathon said they weren't there when he went to his morning class. He had no idea why they were there or what they might signify.

And the present wrapped in birthday paper sitting on Jonathon's night stand (it's his birthday next week). Jonathon opened it. *The Double Helix* by James Watson. The perfect gift for a biology major. It wasn't there when Jonathon got up.

We found ourselves talking about how Arthur could have died. Had he gotten a Dear John letter from home? Was the stress of school too much? Was he terminally ill and knew it? Was this a drug overdose, intentional or accidental? Had he been poisoned? Was it an aneurysm? We discussed in some length whether or not he would have left a note if this were a suicide. We concluded he wouldn't have. Arthur was a very private person.

As I got up to go to my psych class, I walked by the stereo and glanced down to see what record was on the turntable. Bob Dylan's *Nashville Skyline*. "Side B." A morbid, pseudo-detective thought crossed my mind. Did this particular album – correction – did this particular side of this particular album, in any way, reveal additional clues surrounding Arthur's death? I was positive he would have been listening to that album.

I knew Jonathon hated the album ("Dylan sold out," he had claimed when it first came out.), but he obviously hadn't killed Arthur to silence the "country crud" of Bobby.

I told Michael what I was thinking, and we immediately started discussing the album's possible significance.

Jonathon wandered around the apartment looking for other odd things, choosing not to participate in such "stupid conjecture."

Based on the songs on "Side B," there was no doubt in my mind that Arthur had broken up with his girlfriend. Most likely, she had broken up with him. After all, he wrote her all the time and never got a single letter in return. The lyrics supported this, too. "I was so mistaken when I thought she would be true." Also from "One More Night," there was this telling phrase, "Tonight, no light will shed on me." The clincher for me was the next song, "Tell Me It Isn't True." "I don't want to believe them, all I want is your word." He had gotten her word…in the form of a "Dear John" letter. Case closed. Suicide. Broken heart.

In Michael's opinion, it was all about the last song, "Staying Here With You." Maybe Arthur found out he was dying of some disease. Michael said that if we simply listened carefully to the lyrics based on this assumption, it all made sense. "Throw my ticket out the window, throw my suitcase out there, too. Throw my troubles out the door, I don't need them any more." It was all over but the dying. Arthur was finishing up his business. And, to prove it, Michael said, there was this last, telling phrase, "I find it so difficult to leave. I can hear that whistle blowin'. I see that station master, too." Arthur was ready.

We agreed that perhaps it was a combination of both our conjectures. Jonathon then reminded us he knew Arthur best and told us we were nuts. "He just died. It happens." And he left and went for a walk.

Turned out Jonathon was right. Bad heart.

Maybe a broken heart, too. Time for me to buy *Nashville Skyline*.

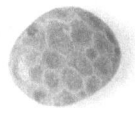

Time Off

He wasn't sure why he started writing it. It wasn't because he could write. And it certainly wasn't because he'd been planning to do it for a long time. It just happened.

He'd come home from work that morning (he worked the 3:30 am to 11:30 am shift). Fed his cat, Mickey. He checked the fridge (even though he knew perfectly well what was in there), changed his clothes, looked out in the barren backyard (if you could call it a backyard) of the old, dilapidated apartment complex he'd called home for the last 15 years. And the next thing he knew, he was writing.

It felt like a short story though he had nothing to compare it to. He wrote for about 30 minutes, stopped, went for a long walk (something else he never did), came home, made himself some Campbell's soup (tomato today) and a baloney and cheese sandwich (he had that a lot), and went to bed. He just lay there for an hour or so, thinking about the world and his place in it (something he'd never done), and then he fell asleep. He got up at 4 pm, wrote for another 30 minutes and went back to sleep. He slept nine hours. Something he couldn't remember doing in all his adult years...and he was no spring chicken.

He woke up fully refreshed. Before he analyzed it, he called in sick at work, something he had never done before. Even when he was sick, he didn't do it.

He went straight from the phone back to his writing, and he wrote for an hour. After a cup of lukewarm instant coffee, he wrote another 15 minutes, went for another walk (this time in the dark), and then read his story out loud. He got a phone call from his concerned line supervisor (he momentarily forgot he'd called in sick but rallied to sound like he was on his death bed), and ate more baloney, more soup (bean and bacon this time), and two Hershey bars with almonds. He had never eaten two Hershey bars at one time. Then he went for another walk and was amazed by all the things he was seeing for the first time. Before he knew it, the day was gone, he was exhausted and ready to turn in.

He was still sick the next day and kept pretty much the same schedule. He finished his story about 8:30 that night, signed it, and celebrated by picking up a pepperoni pizza with extra pepperoni from Lanza's down the street. He even bought a quart of beer. He couldn't remember the last time he'd had a beer.

He had this overpowering desire to tell someone about the story, but he resisted. He could have shown it to his mother, but she'd been dead for years now. To be honest, he couldn't even remember how many years. Then again, there was nothing to tell, really. This wasn't some earth-shattering event. And it would be unbelievable to anyone else. Especially those who "knew" him – or thought they did, because they worked beside him every day.

He went to work the next day as if nothing had happened. His co-workers were glad to see him. Joyce, the receptionist, said they figured he was dying or something since he'd never missed a day of work in 18 years. He thanked them for their concern.

On the way home, he had an odd thought: one day he'd make sure his kids saw his story. He quickly snapped back to reality. He wasn't going to have kids. He barely ever had a date. And that wasn't likely to change.

As he pulled into his parking spot at the apartment, Simon and Garfunkel came on his car radio singing "Richard Corey." He sat there listening to the song. "And wasn't he a most peculiar man." He smiled, turned off the engine, got out of his car, slammed the door with unnecessary force, and hopped up onto the curb. He didn't even bother locking the car door. He always locked his car door.

Mickey greeted him with his raspy voice and led him to the kitchen cabinet next to the stove where the cans of cat food and Campbell's soup were housed. After feeding Mickey, he watched the cat go to the door and ask to be let out. He had never let Mickey outside since the day Mickey showed up at his door.

Until today. He walked over, opened the door and

motioned for Mickey to go out. Mickey looked up at him in total disbelief, then gingerly stepped outside, and, without another thought, quickly bolted off. He knew he would never see Mickey again.

He decided to go bowling, something he hadn't done since he was 16 or 17. He'd been a terrible bowler then, but tonight he got a spare in the first frame and ended up rolling a 155, easily doubling his best score ever.

One game was plenty. He stopped at a drive-through (something he never did) for a burger and fries and gave a dollar to a homeless guy panhandling at the entrance to the restaurant (another first). He drove by the little bookstore in his neighborhood and momentarily considered stopping. He'd never been in it before. And as he passed the local movie theatre, he made a mental note to take in a late show some night. He'd never been there before either.

After eating his meal, he began thinking about what he might write next. Maybe a novel. A scratching sound at the door snapped him out of his reverie. He walked over, opened it up, and in came Mickey, smiling from ear to ear. They had both tempted the world of the unknown and survived. It was time for a beer and an extra can of food for Mickey.

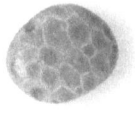

Now!

O n the first day of practice, a chilly March afternoon, I gave my bundled-up track team a pep
talk of sorts about the coming season. I introduced the senior captains (distance runner, Dirk Meyer,
and pole vaulter, Greg Roper), my assistant coaches
(Weaver and Stahl), and reminded the team that they
had less than a month to get in shape, because our first
meet was in early April. And that it was against the
defending conference champs.

Then I let the seniors show the underclassmen the
ropes. I broke them into three groups: sprinters (including the quarter milers, broad jumpers and pole vaulters),
distance runners and half milers, and the other field
event guys. And off they went on my assigned routes.

I thought we would have a good team but certainly
not the best in the conference. We were a team evolving.
Our strengths were in the distances and field events
(shot, high jump, and pole vault), but you don't win a
championship without sprinters, quarter milers, half
milers, and relay teams.

We had some real potential, though. Our freshman

class had some very fast kids, and we had a couple of sophomores ready to step up, too. I'd never depended on underclassmen before, but I was thinking I might give it a try this year. Most of the other coaches in our conference used them. One of the coaches said it made his upperclassmen work harder in practice. Say no more.

I ran the 880 in college so I took the distance group. While they were out running three miles, I walked around, checking the condition of the track and infield, and smiling sadistically to myself, thinking about the poor freshmen getting their indoctrination from Dirk. Normally, the seniors intentionally (and successfully) tried to run the underclassmen into the ground. That was going to be particularly true of Dirk, especially now that he was a captain.

There were 15 in the distance group. Three seniors, three juniors and the rest freshmen and sophomores. Dirk won the mile at the conference meet last year, but got fourth in the regionals and didn't qualify for State. So this year he had a lot to prove. He was a very competitive kid. I'm not sure he was the best all-around role model for the underclassmen, but he sure was intense. Maybe some of that would wear off on his teammates.

After about 30 minutes I saw the first runner coming down Lake Drive toward the west entrance of the track, and naturally assumed it was Dirk. Fifteen seconds later I realized there were two runners, and I was thrilled. It was probably Duncan Bright, a junior who came on strong at the end of last year and should be competitive in the two mile this year.

As they got to the track entrance, on the opposite end of the track from where I was standing, I could definitely tell it was Dirk, but the other guy didn't look like Duncan.

I got distracted momentarily by Coach Stahl yelling something. When I turned back to watch my dynamic duo, I nearly choked. The other runner was one of the freshmen. He was running stride for stride right on Dirk's heels, and from what I could tell, he looked relaxed. If I were a betting man, I would say he had lots left.

The closer they got, the better I could see Dirk's face. He looked pissed at having this kid on his tail. And there was something else. Dirk looked like he was straining. He was tired.

As they came by me, I noticed there was something else about Dirk's expression. It was a shocked look, a look that showed amazement that he was being pushed this hard by a kid. I barked out, "One more lap around, Dirk." And with that, Dirk took off. I knew him well enough to know that this was now war. No underclassman was going to beat him.

It was an amazing final lap to watch. The kid stayed with Dirk step for step, but chose to stay behind him. He never made any attempt to pass, but I had this odd feeling that he could have if he'd wanted to. Dirk kept looking behind him (another sign he was exhausted), hoping that the kid would fade. He didn't, just making Dirk more irritated.

When they finished, Dirk immediately stepped off the track, stopped and bent over, legs shaking, gasping for breath. The kid, looking unfazed by the run, turned around to look for the others. A clump of five or six had just entered the track. Another group was back up on Lake Drive, slowly making their way home.

I walked up to Dirk, patted him on the back and said, "Nice job, Dirk. Great pace." He tried to straighten up, getting about two thirds of the way, and shot me a look like "That wasn't my plan." He glanced toward the kid and just shook his head in disgust.

I went over to the kid and stuck out my hand, "Hey there, I'm Coach K."

"Peter Mullins."

"Peter, nice job out there." By this time, Dirk had come to a fully erect posture again and had joined us, so I didn't say anything else that might piss him off. I wanted to say, "Holy shit, how did you do that, Peter?"

"Welcome to our team, Peter. Do you have any questions for me or Dirk?"

He shook his head, "No, sir. I'm fine."

It just slipped out. "I can see that."

Dirk, totally lacking in even rudimentary communication skills, chose to avoid Peter entirely and spoke to me. "What now, Coach?" But there was a pitiful look in his face that seemed to be pleading, "Don't embarrass me any more today. I don't have it in me."

"Tell you what, Dirk. When the others in your group get here and have had a chance to recover, I want you to walk them around the track twice. And feel free to talk to them about our first meet. Have at it."

The other kids finished. Another freshman, Ricky Jones, had a nice kick at the end to pull away from the last group. I made a mental note to see if he could run the 880 or, dared I dream, the 440.

They walked their laps (I don't think Dirk said a word to them), did some stretching, and then I sent them to the showers. The freshmen walked like a flock of goslings well behind the older boys. Seniority definitely dictated walking order.

The next few weeks went very well. Dirk seemed to mellow a bit. Duncan joined him and Peter on the longer runs. Dirk set the pace, and the other two seemed content to just follow behind. Occasionally, Duncan would run along side him, but never Peter.

The week before our first meet was spring break. I hated that, because it threw my training schedule completely off. Especially for the seniors (and many of the juniors) who, traditionally, went to Florida or the Bahamas or out west skiing. This season was no exception. Even though it was just a week, most of them wouldn't work out and so would have to basically start all over again when they got back. Combine that with the fact that most of the other school's kids stayed home during spring break (and worked out), and you had the perfect recipe for a disaster.

On Thursday night of spring break I got a call from Greg Roper's mom. Greg, my other captain, is the best pole vaulter in our region. I knew it couldn't be good news, and it wasn't. He had broken his right femur skiing at Vail. Freak accident according to her, and I believed her. He wasn't a reckless kid, and things like this happened. All that mattered was he was done for the year.

When I got off the phone, I told my wife I was going for a walk, and she understood completely. I was full of emotions – sadness, anger, frustration, helplessness. I ended up walking three miles to the track. By the time I got there, it was almost totally dark. I figured I'd walk a lap, go back home, and cry myself to sleep.

It was then I noticed someone running on the track. I couldn't tell who it was at first, but within moments I knew. It was Peter Mullins. But there was something different about the way he was running. It was his stride. He wasn't running behind Dirk (who has a short, choppy stride), so he was free to run the way he wanted. And there was one other thing that was different. He was flying around the track.

I didn't want to intrude (and I didn't want him to see me) so I turned around and walked back home. I should have been obsessing about losing Greg for the year, but instead I was re-evaluating tradition and wondering if I had the guts to stick Peter in the mile relay as well as the mile.

He had some things working in his favor. First, none of our sprinters were capable of running the quarter without dying. Second, there were only two legitimate quarter milers. Franks could go 50 flat if he was in shape, and DeWitt was a solid 52-second guy. And only one of the milers or half milers had the speed to do the quarter justice. Dirk. So there was an open slot.

So on Tuesday, the day before the meet, I decided to talk to Peter. I didn't want to give him too much time to think about it and as a result, worry about it. I caught him just before practice.

"Peter, have you got a sec?"

"Yes, sir."

"I want to try something new tomorrow, but I want to be sure you're OK with it."

His facial expression changed ever so slightly. "Sir?"

"I want you to run third leg on the mile relay."

"Sounds good to me, Coach." And he started to leave.

"And –."

He spun around effortlessly and cut me off. "Yes?"

"I have a feeling that you'll be behind when you get the baton. So here's what I'd like to suggest. Catch the guy you're running against as quickly as you can and just ride his butt hard, just like you do with Dirk."

He looked embarrassed.

"Then, in the last 50 to 75 yards, pull out beside him so you can hand the baton off easier. Just stay with him, and I promise you that Franks will win it in the anchor lap."

Peter belted out, "Yes, sir!'

I wasn't done. "And Peter, have fun. If you feel good and want to take off, go right ahead. Fly by that kid like he's standing still. Show him what you've got. Hell, show everyone what you've got."

The meet went well. It was clear we weren't going to win, but I had some pleasant surprises. The two sophomore sprinters looked good. They got fourth and fifth in the 100, and they placed second and third in the 220. And in the 880, we got a first and third. I'd figured we might be lucky to get a third. Ricky Jones, the other freshman I'd noticed that first day of practice, was third.

Then there was the mile. Buddy Grimes, a junior who'd never placed in a meet before, took off like a bat out of hell. He was leading by ten yards after the first lap. However, a hundred yards into the second lap, all the other runners had caught him. They stayed bunched together for the rest of the lap, by which time Buddy looked exhausted. Then, halfway through lap three, it all changed. Four of the runners (Dirk and Peter and two of theirs) made their move, and the others couldn't respond.

So at the three quarter mark it was a four-man race. Then the unexpected happened again. One of their kids, their number one miler from last year, took off. Dirk and Peter went after him with Peter, of course, right behind Dirk. The fourth kid began to fade.

With 300 yards to go, it was a three-way race and, oddly enough, the only thought going through my mind was that I'd never had a freshman distance runner place in a meet. With a little over 220 yards to go, I noticed three critical things. First, Dirk was hurting. The week at the beach hadn't helped. He should have had the race wrapped up by now. The second thing I noticed was that their kid was tired, too, but not as tired as Dirk. I had a feeling he could hold Dirk off.

And then there was Peter. He was running along behind Dirk just as easily as could be. Showing no signs of fatigue. I'm sure he knew what was going on. He had a tough decision to make. Stay behind Dirk and settle for third or take off and win the race.

Before I knew what I was doing, I yelled as loudly as I could, "Go, Peter, it's all yours." Actually, it was more like a scream of joy.

Peter took two strides to the outside and just exploded by them both. Dirk was too tired to react at all, but the other kid, who thought he had the race locked up, came completely undone.

The crowd was stunned. There was a moment of total silence while they digested what had just happened, and then our fans just went nuts.

It was all Peter's race now, and he let it all out. All those weeks of running behind Dirk, trying not to disturb tradition, were behind him now. Having the time of his life running, just like I'd seen him that night on the track. And wearing the biggest smile you've ever seen on a kid's face. He won by a good 15 yards and still looked fresh when he crossed the finish line. Dirk passed the other kid (still in shock from what he had just witnessed) and got second, but looked like he was going to die.

Peter came jogging over to me, still beaming.

"How are you feeling?" I asked him.

Not even particularly winded, he responded, "Fine sir. Just fine."

I had to ask. "When did you know?"

He started talking a mile a minute. "Well sir, to be honest, I could tell Dirk wasn't feeling well after three laps. What I didn't expect though was the other kid taking off like that. So I decided to hang around and just see what happened. Then I heard you and knew it was time. It felt good."

"Did you think you would win?"

"Yes, sir."

"Would you have gone for it if I hadn't yelled at you?"

"I wasn't sure, sir. I wanted to go real bad, but I didn't want to upset Dirk. I had pretty well decided to give him ten more yards when you yelled at me. And you were right. That was the time to go, and so I did."

Ten minutes before the mile relay, Dirk told me his right hamstring was tight and that he was worried about pulling it if he ran. I told him to stretch a little and get some heat on it and not to worry.

I jogged over to Ricky Jones, who had done so well in the half, and told him that he was running the second leg in Dirk's place. He seemed equal parts excited and scared to death.

I'll admit that I can get pretty nervous watching these kids run relays. It's all I can do sometimes to not run onto the track, grab the baton from one of them and take off. But, when the mile relay started, I was as relaxed as I've ever been.

I shouldn't have been. We were going to lose the meet. The best pole vaulter in the region was done for the season, my star miler was going to be a head case for the rest of the year, thanks to a freshman, and my number one hurdler had false started twice and been disqualified, lost his cool and sworn at the starter, and

I knew he would be suspended for the next meet or two.

None of that mattered though. Everyone in the crowd was in for a real treat, and only two people knew it. Peter and I.

Josh DeWitt had a respectable first leg and was only trailing their number one quarter miler by five yards when he handed off to Ricky. Ricky ran out of gas with about 75 yards to go and handed the baton to Peter down a good ten yards. Even so, I thought he did a great job for his first competitive quarter. I knew he'd get better with more practice.

Peter patiently waited for the baton and then did just what I'd told him. He caught the kid in the first 100 yards and settled in right behind him. I was standing in the infield as he came into the final turn with about 110 yards to go, and yelled at the top of my lungs, "Now!"

Peter reacted like he had been shot out of a cannon. He exploded by the kid like he was standing still. And then it looked like he shifted gears again. There were even some gasps from people in the crowd. Peter rocketed down the straightaway, opening up a 15 yard lead easy.

Tommy Franks had never seen a runner come in that strong at the end of a relay leg and so took off early and hard. Their exchange was picture perfect. Tommy got the baton flat out in full stride and never looked back. He added another ten yards to the lead by the time he finished.

When I turned around, Peter and Ricky were being

mobbed by their fellow freshmen. Peter was beaming from ear to ear.

The next four years were going to be a real treat to watch.

About the Author

Jim grew up in East Grand Rapid, Michigan, received his B.A. at Wabash College, M.A. (Anthropology) at the University of North Carolina at Chapel Hill, A.M.L.S at the University of Michigan and M.Ed. (with an emphasis in Environmental Education) at Murray State University. He has had a rewarding career working as an educator and manager for the federal government, teaching at both the high school and university level, running a non-profit organization, and managing a marketing communications' company. Along with his wife, writer/producer Rebecca Reynolds, and writer/director Larry Brand, Jim owns Michigan-based film company, 8180 Films LLC. Their first feature film, CHRISTINA (christinathemovie.com), a post WWII drama based in Berlin and inspired by a true story, stars Nicky Aycox, Jordan Belfi and Stephen Lang. He and Rebecca live in beautiful Leland, Michigan.

www.ingramcontent.com/pod-product-compliance
Lightning Source LLC
Chambersburg PA
CBHW020132180626
46810CB00004B/1522